Publisher:
Wildside Press, LLC

Distributor:
Curtis Circulation

Editor:
John Gregory Betancourt

Associate Editors:
Darrell Schweitzer
Sean Wallace

Assistant Editors:
P.D. Cacek
Diane Weinstein

Adventure Tales is published four times per year by Wildside Press LLC, 9710 Traville Gateway Dr. #234, Rockville, MD 20850. Postmaster & others: send change of address and other subscription matters to Wildside Press, 9710 Traville Gateway Dr. #234, Rockville, MD 20850. Single copies: $7.95 (magazine edition) or $18.95 (book paper edition), postage paid in the U.S.A. Add $2.00 per copy for shipping elsewhere. Subscriptions: four issues for $19.95 in the U.S.A. and its possessions, $29.95 in Canada, and $39.95 elsewhere. All payments must be in U.S. funds and drawn on a U.S. financial institution. If you wish to use PayPal to pay for your subscription, email your payment to: wildside@sff.net.

Tell us what you think! Visit the official *Adventure Tales* message board at:

www.wildsidepress.com

Wildside Press
9710 Traville Gateway Dr.
#234
Rockville, MD 20850
www.wildsidepress.com

CONTENTS

WINTER 2005-2006   Vol. 1, No. 2

Authors: We are looking for interesting new or classic works by authors who originally appeared in the pulp magazines of the early 20th century. No other fiction is desired at this time. We welcome proposals for non-fiction articles on subjects related to pulp magazines.

Illustrators: All artwork is either reprinted from classic pulp magazines or commissioned. We are happy to look at samples (please allow us to keep them for our files) and will assign artwork if and when we have an appropriate project.

WILDSIDE PULP CLASSICS: PULP FACSIMILE SERIES

Series editor: John Gregory Betancourt

#1: *Spicy Mystery Stories* (August 1935)

Includes Robert Leslie Bellem, Atwater Culpepper, Ellery Watson Calder, Carl Moore, E. Hoffman Price, Arthur Wallace, and more.

#2: *Ghost Stories* (June 1931)

Stories by Conrad Richter (author of The Light in the Forest*) and E. & H. Heron featuring psychic detective, Flaxman Low.*

#3: *Spicy Mystery Stories* (February 1937)

Features Robert Leslie Bellem, Lew Merrill (Victor Rousseau) Hugh Speer, Justin Case (Hugh B. Cave), & many others!

#4: *Strange Tales #7* (January 1933)

Features Hugh B. Cave's classic "Murgunstrumm," as well as sto-ries by Robert E. Howard, Henry S. Whitehead, and many more.

#5: *The Black Mask #2* (May 1920)

2nd issue of classic mystery mag, where hardboiled fiction was born!

#6: *Tales of Magic and Mystery* (February 1928)

Legendary rare early fantasy magazine!

#7: *The Phantom Detective #1* (February 1933)

The premiere issue of the detective-hero pulp!

#8: *Submarine Stories* (March 1930)

Rare pulp magazine, stories and articles about (what else?) subs!

#9: *Sinister Stories #1* (Feb 1940)

The first issue of this "weird menace" pulp!

#10: *The Thrill Book* (Sept. 1, 1919)

The facsimile reprint from this legendary rare pulp magazine!

#11: *The Spider* (March 1940)

Includes the "Spider" novel Slaves of the Laughing Death!

#12: *Spicy Adventure Stories* (Dec. 1939)

The Blotter

My favorite convention last year was Rich Harvey's "Pulp Adventurecon," a small (perhaps 100-125 people) gathering of pulp magazine collectors held in Bordentown, New Jersey. The one-day event mostly consisted of people standing around and talking in the dealer's room, where a wide variety of pulp magazines (and books and a few videotapes) were offered for sale. I attended with Sean Wallace, and we had a wonderful time meeting many pen-pals, pulp fans, Wildside Press readers, and of course making new friends. Anyone interested in attending next year's gathering can find information online at Rich Harvey's web site, <www.boldventurepress.com>.

We have a stellar linkup of fiction this issue. Our featured author is the celebrated Nelson Bond, author of hundreds of classic stories, including the Lancelot Biggs series. Although Mr. Bond is no longer active as a writer, he was delighted to be invited to be the Featured Author this issue, and personally selected the work presented here, writing new introductory material and including a previously unpublished poem (originally written in 1939).

Achmed Abdullah is another legendary name from the pulps. His story "Fear" originally appeared in the February 4, 1919 issue of *Detective Story Magazine* and remains one of my personal favorites. (A weekly for many years, *Detective Story Magazine* presented literally thousands of fine early crime and suspense fiction in the United States, with a lineup of dozens of famous contributors . . . though Johnston McCulley, the creator of Zorro, may well be the most remembered today.) For more information on Achmed Abdullah's life, here is an excerpt from an upcoming collection of his work, penned by Darrell Schweitzer:

Achmed Abdullah. There was a time when his name was synonymous with romantic, exotic adventure. The byline of Achmed Abdullah appeared on numerous magazine stories and books. His English style was excellent, even poetic, but with a voice of authenticity that suggested that maybe this writer was an Arab or other "Oriental." All to the better, in an era in which Lawrence of Arabia was one of the first media celebrities and Rudolph Valentino's portrayal of *The Sheik* played to every woman's daydreams.

The truth is more complicated and even more exotic. Those who met Abdullah found him very British in speech, manner, and ideas. Indeed, he had been educated at Eton and Oxford (and the University of Paris), and had served in the British Army in the Middle East, India, and China, but he was actually the son of a Russian Grand Duke, the second cousin of Czar Nicholas II. His Russian name was Alexander Nicholayevitch Romanoff (sometimes given as Romanowski). His Muslim name was Achmed Abdullah Nadir Khan el-Durani el-Iddrissyeh, so, while the byline "Achmed Abdullah" was easy to remember and quite exotic, it wasn't, strictly speaking, a pseudonym, and he came by it legitimately. Admittedly "Achmed Adbullah" was more likely to sell books of Oriental adventure than "Alexander Romanoff."

Abdullah/Romanoff was born in 1881 and died in 1945. His birthplace is variously reported as Malta or Russia. What is certain is that after his army service, he embarked on a general literary career, writing novels and stories of mystery and adventure and some fantasy, with much of his work appearing in the pulp magazines such as *Munsey's, Argosy,* and *All-Story.*

Rounding out this issue are stories by Dorothy Quick, John D. Swain, Harold Lamb, Arthur O. Friel, and Christopher B. Booth. Enjoy!

— *John Gregory Betancourt*

The stories in this issue of *Adventure Tales* originally appeared as follows: "The Black Adder," by Dorothy Quick: *Oriental Stories,* Summer 1932. "Fear," by Achmed Abdullah: *Detective Story Magazine,* February 4, 1919. "Lucifer," by John D. Swain: *Weird Tales,* November 1923. "The Tapir," by Arthur O. Friel: *Adventure,* October 3, 1920. "Mr. Clackworthy's Pot of Gold, by Christopher B. Booth: *Detective Story Magazine,* 1920? "Yellow Elephants," by Harold Lamb: *Argosy,* March 8, 1919. "Shall Stay These Couriers . . .", by Nelson S. Bond: *Thrilling Wonder Stories,* Nov. 1940.

THE BLACK ADDER
by Dorothy Quick

TALFA opened the casement window, and leaning out into the night, tried to see the garden below. It was a quiet, moonless night and she could distinguish nothing. Even the stars were veiled and a heavy impenetrable blue-blackness covered everything. But a soft wind carried the scent of the jasmines to her nostrils.

She knew the garden so well that she could visualize it mentally, although its beauties were hidden from her eyes. There was the crystal pool and beyond it the marble summer house, always cool and inviting. Inside, on the couch of crimson silk, Boud Ali waited. At the thought of him lying there, his slim, muscular body relaxed on the cushions while the black curls of his hair lay loose about his handsome face, Talfa's heart beat faster and her breasts throbbed against the casement sill.

Boud Ali waited for her and her every nerve cried out for him, longed for the relief that only resting in his arms could give. So near he was, such a few short steps and she could feel his lips on hers. Heaven! And yet tonight it could not be!

Talfa shook her head and the two long braids of blue-black hair slipped over the window-ledge, stretching downward into the night. Talfa, like the Fairy Princess of old, had hair that waved softly about her piquant face and then fell rippling downward until it reached her knees. It was very thick and soft and she wore it in braids to keep it out of her way. Her deep brown eyes peered out into the night as though they were striving to see the lover who waited for her, and her red lips trembled a little with the sorrow that enveloped her because she could not go to him.

Just two short weeks they had known each other. Only fourteen days ago she had danced before the Rajah and his guests. Among them had been Boud Ali. As she made the obscene movements that were meant to drive men mad, she had seen him and read desire in his black eyes — desire which had lit a flame in her own heart.

When the dance was over and she and the other dancing-girls lay exhausted on the mosaics of the floor, she had heard the Rajah's voice.

"Choose whom you will among the dancing-girls to be your companion for the night — save those who are virgin: they are for me alone."

Talfa had raised her head and through the clouds of smoke and incense she had seen Boud Ali start toward her. Willingly would she have stayed and given to him all he asked, she who had never known the touch of man. But it was not to be so; for before he ever reached her side, the chief eunuch had caught her by the wrist and led her and two other girls back to the harem.

There slaves had bathed them with scented waters, dried their hair, and they had sought their couches. Only Talfa could not sleep. The black eyes of Boud Ali had haunted her and the heat of the night had been oppressive.

She remembered so well that she had drawn a soft silk mantle over her and stolen silently down to the garden. No guards were about. The garden walls were high and the Rajah unafraid of his women betraying him. They knew too well the penalty that would be theirs if they were caught. For his wives perhaps he kept a stricter watch; but of these Talfa knew nothing, she who had been bought for a concubine because of her beauty and her ability to dance.

For a year she had been in the palace and had never seen the Rajah except on the rare occasions when she was called upon to dance, as she had been tonight. But because she was a virgin, she never was allowed to stay for the aftermath of the feast. The Rajah was generous only with those who no longer tempted him. Talfa knew that some time he would send for her, and then —. But that night she had had no room in her thoughts for anyone beyond Boud Ali.

She had gone down the tiny stairway like a ghost, past the sleeping eunuch, out into the cooling night; beyond the crystal pool she had sought the marble summer house. Here some day she would know the embraces of the Rajah when his eyes would rest upon her with desire. But for tonight she would dream of the young stranger.

As she entered the pavilion someone rose from the crimson couch and came toward her with outstretched hands. In the glow of the moonlight she saw Boud Ali, and a crimson flush stained her slender young body under the silken robe.

Boud Ali spoke, and his voice was low and musical. "Truly the priest spoke well who said we know not the power of our own thoughts. Here have I lain for hours, willing that you should come to me, and so the desire of my life has been granted. You are here!"

Talfa took a step nearer to him. "But how did you come? The walls are far too high to climb."

His clear laugh rang through the scented night. "Nor did I climb! Gold brought me here — gold and a greedy slave, who opened a little-known door in that high wall, and has promised to do so yet again — and will, if you are kind."

The girl moved forward. "I saw you in the banquet hall," she began.

He moved toward her until they stood face to face. "Beloved," he said softly, "I, too, saw such beauty as I had never dreamed, and love was born in my heart. Smile at me, sweet one. Smile, and tell me that I ask not in vain."

Talfa looked deep into his eyes, and the corners of her mouth curved deliciously. With a sudden gesture of surrender, she stretched forth her hands.

The next second she was in his arms and her silken mantle lay unheeded on the floor.

Twice since then the marble summer house had sheltered their love. Gold had truly opened the way for Boud Ali, and Talfa thought little of the risk she ran. She merely waited until the women's house was wrapped in slumber before she stole down the tiny stairway. That death would be her por-

tion if she were discovered, faded away before the magic of her lover's kiss. The fact that the death would be a slow, torturous one, not swift and merciful, she never let come into her thoughts. The moment and Boud Ali were sufficient, and she felt that she would gladly pay any price for the joy, of resting in his arms.

But tonight? Tonight her soul was full of terror, not for herself but for him! They had planned to meet, and her heart had been full of eager anticipation. Then only a few short moments ago word had been brought that the Rajah would visit the women's quarters and that the dancing-girls should be ready to amuse him.

TALFA on hearing the news, had prayed silently that his choice fall not on her when the dance was done. Then like a swift stab of horror had come the thought the Rajah would retire to the summer house with whomever he chose. That was the reason she had seen slaves working there today. They were cleaning and perfuming the pavilion for his use. And just at that time Boud Ali would be there waiting. Death would be his portion, and she could not save him. There was no way. The slave who let him into the garden was in the men's part of the palace; so even if she knew which slave it was, she had no way of reaching him. And she would not dare disclose her secret to anyone who could send a message. Talfa, herself, could neither read nor write. Only fifteen years old, she had been educated solely to attract and interest the senses.

In sheer panic, she had left the other girls, who were chattering like a group of excited monkeys, and had sought this window overlooking the garden. Out there, not very far away, her lover was waiting. What was it he had said of the power of thought? Gods! If only her thoughts could warn him! But she had no faith in her powers of concentration. By all the Gods, there must be a way! Then out of the night and her own despair, an idea was born.

At their last meeting they had laughingly, joked of "The Black Adder," a bandit who had been terrorizing the whole province of Tawnpore, so called because he struck quickly like the reptile, and his touch meant death; also because he was always robed in black with a silk hood over his face. No one had the slightest idea of his identity.

When Talfa had playfully refused one of his caresses, Boud Ali had cried, "Submit, or I will call on the Black Adder to make you. See reason, oh, light of my life!"

And then much later, after she had explained that she had refused only for the joy of giving in, they had spoken of the Black Adder again, and Boud Ali had told her some of the bandit's less gory exploits. Perhaps he would remember their conversation and under cover of a song about the Black Adder she could warn the man she loved. No one hearing would think aught, for the Black Adder's name was on every one's lips.

Of her own fate, should she be the chosen one, she had no time to think. Breathlessly she ran to fetch her lute, and quickly returned to her place by the window. She had little time. Soon she would be called for the ritual of bathing, perfuming and robing that always took place before the arrival of the Rajah.

She struck the first notes softly. Then the music grew louder, the strain that had been played the night she first saw Boud Ali. She leaned far out the window and threw her clear sweet voice out into the night.

"I, Talfa, sing a song of the Black Adder," she repeated over and over, then swung into her song:

"The Black Adder came to the palace of the King.
Within were jewels for his welcoming.
Only the dancing-girl knew waiting was death's sting.
The dancing-girl sang, go away, go away –
The King comes merrily to me this day.
Black Adder, Black Adder, do not dare to stay!
Black Adder, Black Adder, creep into your hole,
Another night brings another goal –
Only tonight would you pay the toll!
Black Adder –"

Her voice died away as she saw the chief eunuch standing beside her. He laughed a shrill, thin laugh that frayed the edge of her nerve.

"Little fool, to sit in the window and sing of the Black Adder when you should be staining your eyes with kohl to snare your lord with their beauty!"

Her lute fell forgotten on the floor as one tiny hand pressed against her heart as though to still its wild beating.

"Come, my pretty one," continued the chief eunuch, as he pulled one of her long braids. "By all the Gods, were I a man, you could make me captive by your hair alone!"

Unresisting, she followed him and passively gave herself into the hands of the women. The fatalism of her race had come to her aid. She had done her best. Now all rested upon the knees of the Gods.

LATER that evening, robed in blue gauze that revealed more than it concealed, with her long hair flowing about her shoulders, she danced with the other girls before the Rajah. Automatically her body moved to the music. Her thoughts were far away, with Boud Ali – hoping.

Suddenly, as the dance brought her near to the couch where the Rajah was lying, she felt the long ends of her hair seized firmly. She stopped writhing and felt herself gently drawn toward the Rajah.

Presently she stood facing him. He held her hair in his firm hands, having pulled it over her shoulder. She felt his eyes pass over her. Somehow she knew fate was upon her and that she would be the chosen one. Trembling, she heard his voice, "Bid the music stop, and send those other girls away." Then she felt his hands upon her, tearing away her robes.

"With hair like that you need no further covering. Come, dance for me, so; and when the dance is over, if you still please me – and fear not but that you will – you shall be honored with my love."

With a slight shudder she shook her hair over her, and of a truth it was more concealing than the blue gauze had been. "A Rajah has no love to give a dancing-girl," she cried, remembering she had only one life to lose.

The Rajah laughed, then his eyes looked into hers. "Perhaps – who knows? – even love! At any rate, tonight you shall be mine. I swear it! Now – dance."

The music started. Automatically Talfa began to move to its rhythm, and then she started to turn and twist in a series of wild convulsions. Another thought had come to her. Perhaps she could so madden and inflame his senses that he would take her here in this room where they were, and Boud Ali would not be discovered in the summer house, if her song had not been heard.

She danced with a furious abandon such as she had never believed herself capable of. If she had drunk of the most potent of aphrodisiacs she could have put no more into her dance.

At last the music came to an end with a loud crash of cymbals, and she fell exhausted at the Rajah's feet.

The Rajah detached the golden robe from his shoulders and threw it over her. Then he came and lifted her into his arms.

"I, myself, will carry you to the pavilion," he cried, his breath coming quickly, his eyes mad with lust.

Two slaves ran before with lighted torches, and the chief eunuch followed behind.

In his arms Talfa lay limply. Soon she would know, and she could hardly bear the suspense. One last effort she would make, for her love's sake. "My lord, why do we not stay here?"

The Rajah made no answer, only strode rapidly on.

Yet another effort she put forth. "Will you not send the men away?"

This time she met with success. "Have no fear. Tonight is yours alone, and tomorrow, and tomorrow, oh lovely one!"

Talfa almost laughed aloud. For her there would be no more tomorrows. When he discovered that another man had spoiled the fruit for him, she had no doubt what her fate would be, unless she could so madden him —

They had reached the pavilion door. The Rajah turned to the slaves. "Put the torches in place and then go — all of you — and come not near until the sun shines brightly from the heavens."

When he had been obeyed, he carried her over the threshold. No one was in the marble summer house!

"Praise to the Gods!" whispered Talfa, and the Rajah hearing, misunderstood, and crushed his lips on hers.

Finally he laid her on the crimson couch and drew away the golden robe. The crimson silk brought out the whiteness of her body. She looked like a living statue as she lay before him.

"Gods!" he cried, "but you are beautiful!" and he moved closer toward her.

All thoughts of submission fled from Talfa. Better death than the embraces of this man. Now that Boud Ali was safe, she was no longer afraid.

She struggled frantically. A cruel gleam came into the Rajah's face, as he pressed her close and sought to force her to comply with his desires.

Just when from sheer exhaustion she could fight no more, she felt the Rajah's arms loosen their hold, and wide-eyed beheld two hands dragging him to his feet.

Forgetful of herself, she looked up. "Gods!" she exclaimed. "The Black Adder!" For holding the Rajah's arms tightly behind his back was a man clothed in black from head to toe with a hood over his face that had slits for eyes and mouth.

The Rajah made a desperate struggle to free himself, but he had been caught off guard and was held by hands of iron.

"What do you want?" he cried finally.

Talfa covered herself with the golden robe before the Black Adder spoke. His voice was muffled by the silken hood, but there was strength in it.

"I had sought your life, oh, Rajah of Tawnpore — your life and your jewels. But even an 'Adder' can be merciful!"

"My guards will give you no mercy," threatened the Rajah in a voice from which he tried vainly to hide his fear.

The Black Adder laughed long and hard. "Think you I am named for nothing? Hidden in the bushes, I heard your order and I waited until the guards had surely gone. Not until the sun is high in the heavens will they come. The Rajah has spoken!"

The ruler of Tawnpore bowed his head. When he finally raised it, he spoke shakily, "Your price?"

The black head leaned over close to the Rajah's. Through the silk, Talfa sensed his eyes upon her and drew her robe closer together over her heaving bosoms.

"I have no price," said the Black Adder. "Yet once I will be merciful. Here, you!" he called to the girl, "tear silken strands from those curtains so that I can bind this man!"

Talfa obeyed silently.

"How dare you?" cried the Rajah.

"Better being bound than dead. I will leave you here on yonder couch and your slaves will release you in the morning. Then you can tell them the Black Adder knows how to be kind."

The Rajah said nothing. Talfa brought the strip of silk to the bandit and under his direction helped to tie the Rajah's hands behind his back.

The Black Adder stretched his arms. "I am afraid," he said softly, "I must rob you of your pearls; and the Ruby of Tawnpore, which I have long envied, will now be mine."

Swiftly he stripped the Rajah of his jewels, which in truth were worth a king's ransom. Working fast, he tied the ruler of Tawnpore securely and laid him on the couch. He bound his body fast about with the crimson silk; then he stuffed a gag into the ruler's mouth and made it fast.

As he finished, Talfa tried to steal toward the doorway and freedom, but swifter than the snake for whom he was named, the man caught her wrist. "Not so — you who are the brightest jewel of all, come with me!"

"No, no!" shrieked Talfa, as he lifted her in his arms.

"Will you come quietly?" he snarled. "Or must I silence you, too?"

Talfa made a gesture of assent. "I have no choice," she whispered.

As he carried her out of the marble summer house that had given her such joy and such misery, Talfa reflected that perhaps it was better this way. At least she was free from the Rajah, and Boud Ali was safe. Perhaps when the Black Adder tired of her, he would set her free; or failing that, if she could find a knife — a strange sense of helplessness descended upon her.

She was conscious that the Black Adder carried her through a low doorway, for he stooped slightly. On the other side were men and horses. A man held her while the bandit mounted an animal as black as himself. Then he leaned over and threw a dark cloak over the Rajah's golden one. She was then lifted up into his arms, and she heard him give the order to ride — and the company moved forth into the night.

They stopped only once, at the outer gates of the palace. Here a paper was given the guards, who let them pass at once. Talfa could see nothing, as the Black Adder had thrown part of the cloak over her head, but she could hear the rustle of the paper.

For a long time they rode furiously. Talfa lost track of time. The swift motion of the horse and the strength of the arms that held her were her last conscious recollections, as she sank into the deep sleep that only comes with exhaustion.

IT WAS light when she opened her eyes. Through the folds of the cloak she could see the sun's rays. She stirred a little.

"Beloved, I thought you would never open your eyes," a well-known voice vibrated in her ears.

Talfa sank back, thinking she dreamed. The cloak was pulled off. The sudden light after the darkness made her blink.

Presently her eyes became accustomed to the light, and she looked up at her captor.

"Boud Ali!" she cried, and touched his smooth face with her hand to see if he were real.

"My little love," he murmured. Then, bending over without slackening his horse's gait, he kissed her fiercely.

Presently they came back to earth. "But how?" asked Talfa. "Where is the Black Adder?"

Boud Ali's free hand dangled a bit of black silk before her eyes. "Here," he cried gayly. "I heard your song and knew the message you meant to convey. So I sought out the Rajah and bade him farewell. He gave me a pass for myself and men. Then I gave a purse of gold to the slave for a key to the garden gate, ostensibly to bid a last farewell to you. After that I waited for the Rajah to bring you to me."

"Suppose he had chosen another?" breathed Talfa.

Her lover laughed. "He could not have, my beautiful! I had my men ready to overpower the guards, but when I heard them dismissed, I sent my men back to the horses, and waited. The rest you know."

"Where are we going?" Talfa asked; not that it mattered, now that she was in her lover's arms. Not even the fact that he was the Black Adder made any difference to her.

"To my home in the Hills. We are quite safe. The Rajah will never know you are Boud Ali's, and together we will find happiness."

"And wealth," added Talfa, remembering the Rajah's jewels. "Only, I shall be afraid when you are off on your expeditions."

"I shall never leave you, now that you are really mine," he promised.

Her laughter rang out like tinkling silver bells. "Then there is the end of the Black Adder!"

Boud Ali shrugged, "Why?"

"If you go forth no more —"

His own mirth drowned hers, "Oh foolish, one, I but played a part for one night, and borrowed a name to gain my love. If I had taken you, the Rajah would have found us out and death would have been our lot. But for the Black Adder he will not look. For my part, I shall think kindly of the bandit that all so abuse."

"And I shall ever bless his name!" cried Talfa as she raised her lips for her lover's kiss.

FEAR

by Achmed Abdullah

THE FACT that the man whom he feared had died ten years earlier did not in the least lessen Stuart McGregor's obsession of horror, of a certain grim expectancy, every time he recalled that final scene, just before Farragut Hutchison disappeared in the African jungle that stood, spectrally motionless as if forged out of some blackish-green metal, in the haggard moonlight.

As he reconstructed it, the whole scene seemed unreal, almost oppressively, ludicrously theatrical. The pall of sodden, stygian darkness all around; the night sounds of soft-winged, obscene things flapping lazily overhead or brushing against the furry trees that held the woolly heat of the tropical day like boiler pipes in a factory; the slimy, swishy things that glided and crawled and wiggled underfoot; the vibrant growl of a hunting lioness that began in a deep basso and peaked to a shrill, high-pitched, ridiculously inadequate treble; a spotted hyena's vicious, bluffing bark; the chirp and whistle of innumerable monkeys; a warthog breaking through the undergrowth with a clumsy, clownish crash — and somewhere, very far away, the staccato thumping of a signal drum, and more faintly yet the answer from the next in line.

He had seen many such drums, made from fire-hollowed palm trees and covered with tightly stretched skin — often the skin of a human enemy.

Yes. He remembered it all. He remembered the night jungle creeping in on their camp like a sentient, malign being — and then that ghastly, ironic moon squinting down, just as Farragut Hutchison walked away between the six giant, plumed, ochre-smeared Bakoto negroes, and bringing into crass relief the tattoo mark on the man's back where the shirt had been torn to tatters by camel thorns and wait-a-bit spikes and saber-shaped palm leaves.

He recalled the occasion when Farragut Hutchison had had himself tattooed; after a crimson, drunken spree at Madam Celeste's place in Port Said, the other side of the Red Sea traders' bazaar, to please a half-caste Swahili dancing girl who looked like a golden Madonna of evil, familiar with all the seven sins. Doubtless the girl had gone shares with the Levantine craftsman who had done the work — an eagle, in bold red and blue, surmounted by a lop-sided crown, and surrounded by a wavy design. The eagle was in profile, and its single eye had a disconcerting trick of winking sardonically whenever Farragut Hutchison moved his back muscles or twitched his shoulder blades.

Always, in his memory, Stuart McGregor saw that tattoo mark.

Always did he see the wicked, leering squint in the eagle's eye — and then he would scream, wherever he happened to be, in a theatre, a Broadway restaurant, or across some good friend's mahogany and beef.

Thinking back, he remembered that, for all their bravado, for all their showing off to each other, both he and Farragut Hutchinson had been afraid since that day, up the hinterland, when, drunk with fermented palm wine, they had insulted the fetish of the Bakotos, while the men were away hunting and none left to guard the village except the women and children and a few feeble old men whose curses and high-pitched maledictions were picturesque, but hardly effectual enough to stop him and his partner from doing a vulgar, intoxicated dance in front of the idol, from grinding burning cigar ends into its squat, repulsive features, and from generally polluting the *juju* hut — not to mention the thorough and profitable looting of the place.

They had got away with the plunder, gold dust and a handful of splendid canary diamonds, before the Bakoto warriors had returned. But fear had followed them, stalked them, trailed them; a fear different from any they had ever experienced before. And be it mentioned that their path of life had been crimson and twisted and fantastic, that they had followed the little squinting swarth-headed, hunch-backed djinni of adventure wherever man's primitive lawlessness rules above the law, from Nome to Timbuktu, from Peru to the black felt tents of Outer Mongolia, from the Australian bush to the absinth-sodden apache haunts of Paris. Be it mentioned, furthermore, that thus, often, they had stared death in the face and, not being fools, had found the staring distasteful and shivery.

But what they had felt on that journey, back to the security of the coast and the ragged Union Jack flapping disconsolately above the British governor's official corrugated iron mansion, had been something worse than mere physical fear; it had been a nameless, brooding, sinister apprehension which had crept through their souls, a harshly discordant note that had pealed through the hidden recesses of their beings.

Everything had seemed to mock them — the crawling, sour-miasmic jungle; the slippery roots and timber falls; the sun of the tropics, brown, decayed, like the sun on the Day of Judgment; the very flowers, spiky, odorous, waxen, un-

11

healthy, lascivious.

At night, when they had rested in some clearing, they had even feared their own campfire — flaring up, twinkling, flickering, then coiling into a ruby ball. It had seemed completely isolated in the purple night.

Isolated!

And they had longed for human companionship — white companionship.

White faces. *White* slang. *White* curses. *White* odors. *White* obscenities.

Why — they would have welcomed a decent, square, honest *white* murder; a knife flashing in some yellow-haired Norse sailor's brawny fist; a belaying pin in the hand of some bullying Liverpool tramp-ship skipper; some Nome gambler's six-gun splattering leaden death; some apache of the Rue de Venise garroting a passerby.

But here, in the African jungle — and how Stuart McGregor remembered it — the fear of death had seemed pregnant with unmentionable horror. There had been no sounds except the buzzing of the tsetse flies and a faint rubbing of drums, whispering through the desert and jungle like the voices of disembodied souls, astray on the outer rim of creation.

And, overhead, the stars. Always, at night, three stars, glittering, leering; and Stuart McGregor, who had gone through college and had once written his college measure of limping, anemic verse, had pointed at them.

"The three stars of Africa!" he had said. "The star of violence! The star of lust! And the little stinking star of greed!"

And he had broken into staccato laughter which had struck Farragut Hutchinson as singularly out of place and had caused him to blurt forth with a wicked curse:

"Shut your trap, you —"

For already they had begun to quarrel, those two pals of a dozen tight, riotous adventures. Already, imperceptibly, gradually, like the shadow of a leaf through summer dusk, a mutual hatred had grown up between them.

But they had controlled themselves. The diamonds were good, could be sold at a big figure; and, even split in two, would mean a comfortable stake.

Then, quite suddenly, had come the end — the end for them.

And the twisting, gliding skill of Stuart McGregor's fingers had made sure that Farragut Hutchison should be that one.

Years after, when Africa as a whole had faded to a memory of coiling, unclean shadows, Stuart McGregor used to say, with that rather plaintive, monotonous drawl of his, that the end of this phantasmal African adventure had been different from what he had expected it to be.

In a way, he had found it disappointing.

Not that it had lacked in purely dramatic thrills and blood-curdling trimmings. That wasn't it. On the contrary, it had had a plethora of thrills.

But, rather, he must have been keyed up to too high a pitch; must have expected too much, feared too much during that journey from the Bakoto village back through the hinterland.

Thus when, one night, the Bakoto warriors had come from nowhere, out of the jungle, hundreds of them, silent, as if the wilderness had spewed them forth, it had seemed quite prosy.

Prosy, too, had been the expectation of death. It had even seemed a welcome relief from the straining fatigues of the jungle pull, the recurrent fits of fever, the flying and crawling pests, the gnawing moroseness which is so typically African.

"An explosion of life and hatred," Stuart McGregor used to say, "that's what I had expected, don't you see? Quick and merciless. And it wasn't. For the end came — slow and inevitable. Solid. Greek in a way. And *so* courtly! *So* polite! That was the worst of it!"

For the leader of the Bakotos, a tall, broad, frizzy, odorous warrior, with a face like a black Nero with a dash of Manchu emperor, had bowed before them with a great clanking of barbarous ornaments. There had been no marring taint of hatred in his voice as he told them that they must pay for their insults to the fetish. He had not even mentioned the theft of the gold dust and diamonds.

"My heart is heavy at the thought, white chiefs," he said. "But — you must pay!"

Stuart McGregor had stammered ineffectual, foolish apologies:

"We — we were drunk. We didn't know what — oh — what we —"

"What you were doing!" the Bakoto had finished the sentence for him, with a little melancholy sigh. "And there is forgiveness in my heart —"

"You — you mean to say —" Farragut Hutchison had jumped up, with extended hand, blurting out hectic thanks.

"Forgiveness in *my* heart, not the *juju*'s," gently continued the negro. "For the *juju* never forgives. On the other hand, the *juju* is fair. He wants his just measure of blood. Not an ounce more. Therefore," the Bakoto had gone on, and his face had been as stony and as passionless as that of the Buddha who meditates in the shade of the cobra's hood, "the choice will be yours."

"Choice?" Farragut Hutchison had looked up, a gleam of hope in his eyes.

"Yes. Choice which one of you will die." The Bakoto had smiled, with the same suave courtliness which had, somehow, increased the utter horror of the scene. "Die — oh — a slow death, befitting the insult to the *juju*, befitting the *juju*'s great holiness!"

Suddenly, Stuart McGregor had understood that there would be no arguing, no bargaining whatsoever; and, quickly, had come his hysterical question:

"Who? I – or –"

He had slurred and stopped, somehow ashamed, and the Bakoto had finished the interrupted question with gentle, gliding, inhuman laughter: "Your friend? White chief, that is for you two to decide. I only know that the *juju* has spoken to the priest, and that he is satisfied with the life of one of you two; the life – and the death. A slow death."

He had paused; then had continued gently, so very, very gently: "Yes. A slow death, depending entirely upon the vitality of the one of you two who will be sacrificed to the *juju*. There will be little knives. There will be the flying insects which follow the smell of blood and festering flesh. Too, there will be many crimson-headed ants, many ants – and a thin river of honey to show them the trail."

He had yawned. Then he had gone on: "Consider. The *juju* is just. He only wants the sacrifice of one of you, and you yourselves must decide which one shall go, and which one shall stay. And – remember the little, little knives. Be pleased to remember the many ants which follow the honey trail. I shall return shortly and hear your choice."

He had bowed and, with his silent warriors, had stepped back into the jungle that had closed behind them like a curtain.

Even in that moment of stark, enormous horror, horror too great to be grasped, horror that swept over and beyond the barriers of fear – even in that moment Stuart McGregor had realized that, by leaving the choice to them, the Bakoto had committed a refined cruelty worthy of a more civilized race, and had added a psychic torture fully as dreadful as the physical torture of the little knives.

Too, in that moment of ghastly, lecherous expectancy, he had known that it was Farragut Hutchison who would be sacrificed to the *juju* – Farragut Hutchison who sat there, staring into the camp fire, making queer little, funny noises in his throat.

Suddenly, Stuart McGregor had laughed – he remembered that laugh to his dying day – and had thrown a greasy pack of playing cards into the circle of meager, indifferent light.

"Let the cards decide, old boy," he had shouted. "One hand of poker – and no drawing to your hand. Showdown! That's square, isn't it?"

"Sure!" the other had replied, still staring straight ahead of him. "Go ahead and deal –"

His voice had drifted into a mumble while Stuart McGregor had picked up the deck, had shuffled, slowly, mechanically.

As he shuffled, it had seemed to him as if his brain was frantically telegraphing to his fingers, as if all those delicate little nerves that ran from the back of his skull down to his finger tips were throbbing a clicking little chorus:

"*Do – it – Mac! Do – it – Mac! Do – it – Mac!*" with a mad-

dening, syncopated rhythm.

And he had kept on shuffling, had kept on watching the motions of his fingers – and had seen that his thumb and second finger had shuffled the ace of hearts to the bottom of the deck.

Had he done it on purpose? He did not know then. He never found out – though, in his memory, he lived through the scene a thousand times.

But there were the little knives. There were the ants. There was the honey trail. There was his own, hard decision to live. And, years earlier, he had been a professional faro dealer at Silver City.

Another ace had joined the first at the bottom of the deck. The third. The fourth.

And then Farragut Hutchison's violent: "Deal, man, deal! You're driving me crazy. Get it over with."

The sweat had been pouring from Stuart McGregor's face. His blood had throbbed in his veins. Something like a sledgehammer had drummed at the base of his skull.

"Cut, won't you?" he had said, his voice coming as if from very far away.

The other had waved a trembling hand, "No, no! Deal 'em as they lie. You won't cheat me."

Stuart McGregor had cleared a little space on the ground with the point of his shoe.

He remembered the motion. He remembered how the dead leaves had stirred with a dry, rasping, tragic sound, how something slimy and phosphorous-green had squirmed through the tufted jungle grass, how a little furry scorpion had scurried away with a clicking *tchk-tchk-tchk*.

He had dealt.

Mechanically, even as he was watching them, his fingers had given himself five cards from the bottom of the deck. Four aces – and the queen of diamonds. And, the next second, in answer to Farragut Hutchison's choked: "Showdown! I have two pair – kings – and jacks!" his own well simulated shriek of joy and triumph:

"I win! I've four aces! Every ace in the pack!"

And then Farragut Hutchison's weak, ridiculous exclamation – ridiculous considering the dreadful fate that awaited him:

"Geewhittaker! You're some lucky guy, aren't you, Mac?"

At the same moment, the Bakoto chief had stepped out of the jungle, followed by half a dozen warriors.

Then the final scene – that ghastly, ironic moon squinting down, just as Farragut Hutchison had walked away between the giant, plumed, ochre-smeared Bakoto negroes, and bringing into stark relief the tattoo mark on his back where the shirt had been torn to tatters – and the leering, evil wink in the eagle's eye as Farragut Hutchison twitched his shoulder blades with absurd, nervous resignation.

Stuart McGregor remembered it every day of his life.

He spoke of it to many. But only to Father Aloysius

O'Donnell, the priest who officiated in the little Gothic church around the corner, on Ninth Avenue, did he tell the whole truth — did he confess that he had cheated.

"Of course I cheated!" he said. "Of course!" And, with a sort of mocking bravado: "What would you have done, padre?"

The priest, who was old and wise and gentle, thus not at all sure of himself, shook his head.

"I don't know," he replied. "I don't know."

"Well — I *do* know. You would have done what I did. You wouldn't have been able to help yourself." Then, in a low voice: "And you would have paid! As I pay — every day, every minute, every second of my life."

"Regret, repentance," murmured the priest, but the other cut him short.

"Repentance — nothing. I regret nothing! I repent nothing! I'd do the same tomorrow. It isn't that — oh — that — what d'ye call it — sting of conscience, that's driving me crazy. It's fear!"

"Fear of what?" asked Father O'Donnell.

"Fear of Farragut Hutchison — who is dead!"

TEN YEARS AGO!

And he knew that Farragut Hutchison had died. For not long afterward a British trader had come upon certain gruesome but unmistakable remains and had brought the tale to the coast. Yet was there fear in Stuart McGregor's soul, fear worse than the fear of the little knives. Fear of Farragut Hutchison who was dead?

No. He did not believe that the man was dead. He did not believe it, could not believe it.

"And even suppose he's dead," he used to say to the priest, "he'll get me. He'll get me as sure as you're born. I saw it in the eye of that eagle — the squinting eye of that infernal, tattooed eagle!"

Then he would turn a grayish yellow, his whole body would tremble with a terrible palsy and, in a sort of whine, which was both ridiculous and pathetic, given his size and bulk, given the crimson, twisted adventures through which he had passed, he would exclaim:

"He'll get me. He'll get me. He'll get me even from beyond the grave."

And then Father O'Donnell would cross himself rapidly, just a little guiltily.

It is said that there is a morbid curiosity which forces the murderer to view the place of his crime.

Some psychic reason of the same kind may have caused Stuart McGregor to decorate the walls and corners of his sitting room with the memories of that Africa which he feared and hated, and which, daily, he was trying to forget — with a shimmering, cruel mass of jungle curios, sjamboks and assegais, signal drums and daggers, knobkerries and rhino shields and what not.

Steadily, he added to his collection, buying in auction rooms, in little shops on the waterfront, from sailors and ship pursers and collectors who had duplicates for sale.

He became a well-known figure in the row of antique stores in back of Madison Square Garden, and was so liberal when it came to payment that Morris Newman, who specialized in African curios, would send the pick of all the new stuff he bought to his house.

IT WAS on a day in August — one of those tropical New York days when the very birds gasp for air, when orange-flaming sun rays drop from the brazen sky like crackling spears and the melting asphalt picks them up again and tosses them high — that Stuart McGregor, returning from a short walk, found a large, round package in his sitting room.

"Mr. Newman sent it," his servant explained. "He said it's a rare curio, and he's sure you'll like it."

"All right."

The servant bowed, left, and closed the door, while Stuart McGregor cut the twine, unwrapped the paper, looked.

And then, suddenly, he screamed with fear; and, just as suddenly, the scream of fear turned into a scream of maniacal joy.

For the thing which Newman had sent him was an African signal drum, covered with tightly stretched skin-human skin — white skin! And square in the center there was a tattoo mark — an eagle in red and blue, surmounted by a lopsided crown, and surrounded by a wavy design.

Here was the final proof that Farragut Hutchison was dead, that, forever, he was rid of his fear. In a paroxysm of joy, he picked up the drum and clutched it to his heart.

And then he gave a cry of pain. His lips quivered, frothed. His hands dropped the drum and fanned the air, and he looked at the thing that had fastened itself to his right wrist.

It seemed like a short length of rope, grayish in color, spotted with dull red. Even as Stuart McGregor dropped to the floor, dying, he knew what had happened.

A little venomous snake, an African fer-de-lance, that had been curled up in the inside of the drum, been numbed by the cold, and had been revived by the splintering heat of New York.

Yes — even as he died he knew what had happened. Even as he died, he saw that malign, obscene squint in the eagle's eye. Even as he died, he knew that Farragut Hutchison had killed him — from beyond the grave!

LUCIFER
by John D. Swain

THE NOTORIOUS Remsen Case was table-talk a year or so ago, although a few today could quote the details offhand. Because of it, half a dozen men were discussing psychic trivialities, in a more or less desultory way. Bliven, the psychoanalyst, was speaking.

"It all hinges on a tendency which is perhaps best expressed in such old saws as: 'Drowning men clutch at straws,' 'Any port in a storm,' or, 'A gambling chance.'

"When men have exhausted science and religion, they turn to mediums, and crystal-gazers, and clairvoyants, and patent medicines. I knew an intelligent pharmacist who was dying of a malignant disease. Operated on three times. Specialists had given him up. Then he began to take the nostrums and cure-alls on his own shelves, although he knew perfectly well what they contained — or could easily enough have found out. Consulted a lot of herb doctors, and long-haired Indian healers, and advertising specialists."

"And, of course, without result," commented the little English doctor.

"I wouldn't say that," said Bliven. "It kept alive the forlorn spark of hope in his soul. Better than merely folding his hands and waiting for the inevitable! He was just starting in with a miraculous Brazilian root, when he snuffed out. On the whole, he lived happier, and quite possibly longer, because of all the fake remedies and doctors he spent so much money on. It's all in your own mind, you know. Nothing else counts much."

"All fakes, including the records of the P.S.R.," nodded Holmes, who lectured on experimental psychology.

The little doctor shook his head depreciatingly.

"I shouldn't go as far as that, really," he objected, "because, every now and then, in the midst of their conscious faking, as you call it, with the marked cards and prepared slates, the hidden magnets and invisible wires and all, these mediums and pseudo-magicians come up against something that utterly baffles them. I have talked with a well-known prestidigitator who has a standing bet of a hundred guineas that he can duplicate the manifestations of any medium; and yet he states that every now and then he finds himself utterly baffled. He can fake the thing cleverly, you understand; but he cannot fathom the unknown forces back of it all. It is dangerous ground. It is sometimes blasphemy! It is blundering in where angels fear to tread."

"Piffle!" snorted Bliven. "The subconscious mind explains it all; and we have only skirted the edge of our subject. When we have mastered it, we shall do thing right in the laboratory that will put every astrologer and palmist and tea-ground prophet out of business."

Nobody seemed to have anything to answer, and the psychoanalyst turned to the little doctor.

"You know this, Royce," he asserted, a bit defiantly.

"I don't pretend to follow you new-era chaps as closely as I ought; but I recall an incident in my early practice that is not explicable in the present-day stage of your science, as I understand it."

Bliven grunted.

"Well — shoot!" he said, "Of course, we can't check up your facts, but if you were an accurate observer, we may be able to offer a plausible theory, at least."

Royce flushed at his brusque way of putting it, but took no offence. Everyone makes allowances for Bliven, who is a good fellow, but crudely sure of himself, and a slave to his hobby.

"It happened a long, long time ago," began Royce, "when I was an interne in a London hospital. If you know anything about our hospitals, you will understand that they are about the last places on earth for anything bizarre to occur in. Everything is frightfully ethical, and prosy, and red-tapey — far more so than in institutions over here, better as these are in many ways.

"But almost anything can happen in London, and does. You love to point to New York as the typical Cosmopolis — because it has a larger Italian population than has Rome, a larger German than Berlin, a Jewish than Jerusalem, and so forth. Well, London has all this, and more. It has nuclei of Afghans, and Turkomans, and Arabs; it has neighborhoods where conversation is carried on in no known tongue. It even has a Synagogue of Negro Jews — dating certainly from the Plantagenet dynasty, and probably earlier.

"Myriads spend all their lives in London, and die knowing nothing about it. Sir Walter Besant devoted twenty years to the collecting of data for his history of the city, and confessed that he had only a smattering of his subject. Men learn some one of its hundred phases passing well; Scotland Yard agents, buyers of old pewter or black-letter books, tea importers, hotel keepers, solicitors, clubmen; but outside of their own little broods the eternal fog, hiding the real London in its sticky, yellow embrace. I was born there, attended its University, practiced for a couple of years in Whitechapel, and migrated to the fashionable Westminster district; but I visit the city as a stranger.

"So, if anything mysterious were to happen anywhere, it might well be in London; although as I have said, one would hardly look for it in one of our solid, dull, intensely prosaic hospitals.

"Watts-Bedloe was the big man in my day. You will find his works in your medical libraries, Bliven; though I dare say he has been thrust aside by the onmarch of science. Osteopathy owes a deal to him, I think; and I know that Doctor Lorenz, the great orthopedist of today, freely acknowledges his own debt.

"There was brought to us one day a peculiarly distressing case; the only child of Sir William Hutchinson, a widower, whose hopes had almost idolatrously centered in this boy, who was a cripple. You would have to be British to understand just how Sir William felt. He was a keen sportsman; played all outdoor games superlatively well, rode to hounds over his own fields, shot tigers from an elephant's back in India, and on foot in Africa, rented a salmon stream in Norway, captained the All-English polo team for years, sailed his own yacht, bred his own hunters, had climbed all the more difficult Swiss peaks, and was the first amateur to operate a biplane.

"So that to natural parental grief was added the bitter downfall of all the plans he had for this boy; instructing him in the fine art of fly-casting, straight shooting, hard riding, and all that sort of thing. Instead of a companion who could take up the life of his advancing years were forcing him to relinquish, in a measure, he had a hopeless cripple to carry on, and end his line.

"He was a dear, patient little lad, with the most beautiful head, and great, intelligent eyes; but his wretched little body was enough to wring your heart. Twisted, warped, shriveled — and far beyond the skill of Watts-Bedloe himself, who had been Sir William's last resort. When he sadly confessed that there was nothing he could do, that science and skillful nursing might add a few years to the mere existence of the little martyr, you will understand that his father came to that pass which you, Bliven, have illustrated in citing the case of the pharmacist. He was, in short, ready to try anything: to turn to quacks, necromancers, to Satan himself, if his son might be made whole!

"Oh, naturally he had sought the aid of religion. Noted clergy of his own faith had anointed the brave eyes, the patient lips, the crooked limbs, and prayed that God might work a miracle. But none was vouchsafed. I haven't the least idea who it was that suggested the to Luciferians to Sir William."

"Luciferians? Devil worshipers?" interrupted Holmes. "Were there any of them in your time?"

"There are plenty of them today; but it is the most secret sect in the world. Huysmand in La-Bas has told us as much as has anyone; and you know perfectly well, or should, that all priests who believe in the Real Presence, take the utmost care that the sacred wafer does not pass into irresponsible hands. Many will not even place it on the communicant's palm; but only in his mouth. For the stolen Host is essential to the celebration of the infamous Black Mass which forms the chief ceremony of the Luciferian ritual. And every year a number of thefts, or attempted thefts, from the tabernaculum, are reported in the press.

"Now the theory of this strange sect is not without a certain distorted rationality. They argue that Lucifer's Star of the Morning was cast out of Heaven after a great battle, in which he was defected to be sure, but not destroyed, nor even crippled. Today, after centuries of missionary zeal, Christianity has gathered only a tithe of the people into its fold; the great majority is, and always has been, outside. The wicked flourish, often the righteous stumble; and at the last great battle of Armageddon, the Luciferians believe that their champion will finally triumph.

"Meanwhile, and in almost impenetrable secrecy, they practice their infamous rites and serve the devil, foregathering preferably in some abandoned church, which has an altar, and above it a crucifix, which they reverse. It is believed that they number hundreds of thousands, and flourish in every quarter of the world; and it is presumed that they employ grips and passwords. But amid so much that is conjecture, this fact stands clear: the cult of Lucifer does exist, and has from time immemorial.

"I never had the least idea who suggested them to Sir William. May have been some friend who was a secret devotee, and wished to make a proselyte. Nay have been an idle word overheard in a club — or penny bus. The point is, he did hear, discovered that an occult power was claimed by their unholy priests, was ready to mortgage his estate or sell his soul for this little chap, and somehow got in touch with them.

"The fact that he managed it, that he browbeat Watts-Bedloe into permitting one of the fraternity to enter the hospital at all, is the best example I an give of his despairing persistence. At that, the physician agreed only upon certain seemingly prohibitive conditions. The fellow was not to touch the little patient, nor even to draw near his bed. He was not to speak to him, or seek to hold his gaze. No phony hypnotism, or anything like that.

"Watts-Bedloe, I think, framed the conditions in the confident hope that they would end negotiations; and he was profoundly disgusted when he learned that the Luciferian, though apathetic, was not in the least deterred by the hardness of the terms. It appeared that he had not been at all willing to come under any circumstances; that he tried persistently to learn how Sir William had heard of him, and his address, and that he had refused remuneration of any sort. Altogether, a new breed of fakir, you see!

"There were five of us in the room at the time appointed,

besides the little patient, who was sleeping peacefully. Fact is, Watts-Bedloe had taken the precaution of administering a sleeping draught, in order that the quack might not in any possible way work upon his nervous system. Watts-Bedloe was standing by the cot, his sandy hair rumpled, his stiff moustache bristling, for all the world like an Airdale terrier on guard. The father was there, of course; and the head nurse, and a powerful and taciturn orderly. You can see that there wasn't much chance of the devil-man pulling off anything untoward!

"When, precisely on the moment, the door opened and he stood before us, I suffered as great a shock of surprise as ever in my life; and a rapid glance at my companions' faces showed me that their amazement equaled mine. I don't know just what type we had visualized — whether a white-bearded mystic clad in a long cloak with a peaked hat bearing cabalistic symbols, or a pale, sinister and debonair man of the world, such as George Arliss has given us, or what not; but certainly not the utterly insignificant creature who bowed awkwardly, and stood twirling a bowler hat in his hands as the door closed behind him.

"He was a little, plump, bald man of middle age, looking for all the world like an unsuccessful greengrocer, or a dealer in butter and cheese in a small way. Although the day was cool, with a damp yellow fog swirling over the city, he perspired freely, and continually wiped his brow with a cheap bandana. He seemed at once ill at ease, yet perfectly confident, if you know what I mean. I realize that it sounds like silly rot; but that is the only way I can describe him. Utterly certain that he could do that for which he had come, but very much wishing that he were anywhere else. I heard Watts-Bedloe mutter 'my word!' And I believe he would have spat disgustedly — were such an act thinkable of a physician in a London hospital!

"The Luciferian priest turned to Sir William. When he spoke, it seemed entirely in keeping with his appearance that he should take liberties with his aspirates. 'I'm 'ere, m'lord. And h'at your service.'

"Watts-Bedloe spoke sharply, 'Look here, my man!' he said. 'Do you pretend to say that you can make this crippled child whole?'

"The strange man turned his moist, pasty face, livid in the fog murk, toward the specialist. 'E that I serves can, and will. I'm a middleman, in a manner of speaking. A transmitter. H'its easy enough for 'im, but I don't advise it, and I warns you I'm not to be 'eld responsible for 'ow 'E does it.'

"Watts-Bedloe turned to Sir William. 'Let's have an end to the sickening farce,' he said curtly. 'I need fresh air!'

"Sir William nodded to the little man, who mopped his brow with his bandana, and pointed to the cot. 'Draw back the coverlet!' he commanded.

"The nurse obeyed, after a questioning glance at Watts-Bedloe. 'Tyke off 'is night gown,' continued the visitor.

"Watts-Bedloe's lips parted in a snarl at this, but Sir William arrested him with a gesture, stepped to his son's side, and with infinite gentleness took off the tiny gown, leaving the sleeping child naked in his bed.

"Again, as always, I felt a surge of pity sweep through me. The noble head, the pigeon breast, rising and falling softly now, the crooked spine, the little gnarled, twisted limbs! But my attention was quickly drawn back to the strange man.

"Barely glancing at the child, he fumbled at his greasy waistcoat, Watts-Bedloe watching him meanwhile like a lynx, as he took out a crumb of chalk and, squatting down, drew a rude circle on the floor about him; a circle of possibly four feet in diameter. And within this circle he began laboriously to write certain works and figures."

"Hold on there!" spoke Bliven. "Certain words and figures? Just what symbols, please?"

"There was a swastika emblem," Royce promptly replied, "and others familiar to some of the older secret orders, and sometimes found on Aztec ruins and Babylonian brick tablets; the open eye, for instance, and a rude fist with thumb extended. Also he scrawled the sequence 1-2-3-4-5-6-7-9, the '8' omitted, you notice, which he multiplied by 18, and again by 27, and by 36; you can amuse yourselves working it out. The result is curious. Lastly, he wrote the sentence, 'Sigma te, sigma, temere me tangis et angis.' A palindrome, you observe; that is, it reads equally well — or ill, backward or forward."

"Hocus pocus! Old stuff!" snorted Bliven.

Royce gazed mildly at him.

"Old stuff, as you say, professor. Older than recorded history. Having done this, a matter of five minutes, perhaps, with Watts-Bedloe becoming more and more restless, and evidently holding himself in with difficulty, the fellow rose stiffly from his squatting position, carefully replaced the fragment of chalk in his pocket, mopped his brow for the twentieth time, and gestured toward the cot with a moist palm. 'Now, cover 'im h'up!' he ordered. 'All h'up; 'ead and all.'

"The nurse gently drew the sheet over the little form. We could see it rise and fall with the regular respiration of slumber. Suddenly, eyes wide open and staring at the floor, the fellow began to pray, in Latin. And whatever his English, his Latin was beautiful to listen to, and virgin pure! It was too voluble for me to follow verbatim — I made as good a transcript as I could a bit later, and will be glad to show it to you, Bliven — but, anyhow, it was a prayer to Lucifer, at once an adoration and a petition, that he would vouchsafe before these Christian unbelievers a proof of his dominion over fire, earth, air and water. He ceased abruptly as he had begun, and nodded toward the cot. 'H'it is done!' he sighed, and once again mopped his forehead.

"'You infernal charlatan!' snarled Watts-Bedloe, unable longer to contain himself. 'You've got the effrontery to stand there and tell us anything has been wrought upon that child by your slobbering drivel?'

"The man looked at him with lusterless eyes. 'Look for yerself, guv'ner.' he answered.

"It was Sir William who snatched back the sheet from his son; and till my dying day I shall remember the unearthly beauty of what our astounded eyes beheld. Lying there, smile upon his lips, like a perfect form fresh from the hand of his Creator, his little limbs straight and delicately rounded, a picture of almost awesome loveliness, lay the child we had but five minutes before seen as a wrecked and broken travesty of humanity."

Again Bliven interrupted explosively:

"Oh, I say now, Royce! I'll admit you tell a ripping story, as such; you had even me hanging breathless on your climax. But this is too much! As man to man, you can't sit there and tell us this child was cured!"

"I didn't say that; for he was dead."

Bliven was speechless, for once; but Holmes spoke up in remonstrance:

"It seems strange to me that such a queer story should not have been repeated, and discussed!"

"It isn't strange, if you happen to know anything about London hospitals," Royce explained patiently. "Who would repeat it? Would Watts-Bedloe permit it to be known that by his permission some charlatan was admitted, and that during his devilish incantations his patient died? Would the stricken father mention the subject, even to us? Or the head nurse and orderly, cogs in an inexorable machine?

"All this took place nearly forty years ago; and it is the first time I have spoken of it. Watts-Bedloe died years back; and Sir William's line is extinct. I can't verify a detail; but it all happened exactly as I have stated. As for the Luciferians, none of us, I think, saw him depart. He simply stole out into the slimy yellow fog, back to whatever private hell it was he came from, somewhere in London, the city nobody knows, and where anything may happen!"

MR. CLACKWORTHY'S POT OF GOLD
by Christopher B. Booth

Although the relaxed posture of his body suggested indolent ease as he reclined in the depths of a luxuriously comfortable, overstuffed chair, Mr. Amos Clackworthy's shrewd brain was exceedingly active. Between his eyebrows there was a faint frown, and the eyes themselves lacked that whimsical twinkle which so often accompanied the incubation of a scheme, one of those clever ideas of his, calculated to swell the Clackworthy bank balance to the corresponding diminishment of someone else's.

The truth of it was that the master confidence man's mind, while diligently in pursuit of that alluring coinage called "easy money," was only running around in circles, starting at nowhere and arriving at precisely the same place. Even a master confidence man's fund of originality must run low at times.

Occupying his favorite place by the window which looked out upon Sheridan Road, Mr. James Early, otherwise "The Early Bird," tapped the toes of his shoes soundlessly on the thick nap of the beautiful Chinese rug of blue and gold, woven together in a perfect harmony of shading. For more than an hour he had kept his peace, but not without many anxious glances toward the meditative Mr. Clackworthy.

"What's the matter, boss?" he demanded at length. "Ain'tcha able to coax an idear from the ol' bean? Mebbe if you primed the think-cylinders with a li'le joy-juice now—"

"It is the weather, James." The master confidence man sighed in admission of his discouragement. "The heat has gotten next to me, it seems." His hand reached out and tapped the card-index file, a neat little compartment of exquisitely polished rosewood matching the table; it contained the names of various men well rated financially, selected as future contributors to Mr. Clackworthy's income. There was an amazing lot of information in those brief notations, intimate data which would have surprised and dumfounded the subjects thereof; their foibles, hobbies, and, not uncommonly, the secret chapters of their lives. The rosewood file was a "prospect list," a methodical arrangement kept by the man who made the pursuit of easy money a thorough and profitable business.

"Not a single hunch," he murmured. "It seems to be the closed season for my pet list of suckers, and—"

"An' it don't take no movin' van to tote the bankroll," interrupted The Early Bird quickly. "Ain't that it?" His voice took on an apprehensive inflection, but Mr. Clackworthy smiled reassuringly.

"We can hardly go into competition with the sub-treasury," he admitted, "but neither are we in the imminent danger of becoming public charges. The bank balance, to speak in the concrete terms of dollars and cents, is precisely" — he turned to a penciled memo at his elbow — "nineteen thousand two hundred and sixty-three dollars thirty-three cents. In some respects a reassuring sum, but it must be remembered that a confidence man can't expect to win much confidence without a good and sufficient working capital. The sight of a neat little packet of thousand-dollar bills is more convincing than all the logic; the man who needs credit the worst has the hardest time getting it. Money is the magnate which —"

"Nix on the essay," interrupted The Early Bird ruefully; "work the chin a little less an' the noodle a little harder, boss. If the sum total of our mutual assets ain't more'n nineteen thousand two hundred an' sixty-three berries — me bein' flat, due to payin' tuition in gettin' educated to the fact that a full house ain't always worth the limit — we gotta get busy an' garner in some kale. Lately, things ain't been breakin' right for You, Us an' Company, Unincorporated."

"Yes, we've had a rotten run of luck, James," admitted Mr. Clackworthy. "If I were superstitious, perhaps I would say that an evil jinx has been clogging our footsteps."

"Huh!" snorted The Early Bird. "I hope you ain't got the notion that we've been operatin' under the guidance of a lucky star. Three flivvers out of five schemes, an' on them two we did put over you can't say that we took enough coin outta circulation to start the mint workin' overtime. I'll tell the money-worshipin' world we didn't!"

"At least we stayed out of jail," reminded Mr. Clackworthy. "That much was lucky." The Early Bird shivered at the forced recollection of their narrow escape from durance vile; Mr. Clackworthy had played too far across the legal line and had almost come to grief.

"There was a guy what once spieled 'Money talks,'" said The Early Bird, hastily changing the subject. "I sure make the wish that it would murmur a sweet li'le lovesong into our eagerly strainin' ears; somethin' like 'I'd leave my happy home for you.' As it is, we ain't even heard it whisper."

Mr. Clackworthy laughed, his coplotter's idiomatic humor restoring his genial good nature. He reached across the table to his cigar humidor and selected one of his favorite brand of perfectos.

"That suggestion of yours, James, about appealing to Bacchus' for an idea to fertilize the sterility of our brains, and —"

"What mob does this Bacchus guy train with?" demanded The Early Bird. "I ain't strong for cuttin' in no outsiders."

"My dear James!" remonstrated the master confidence man." Your ignorance of mythology is appalling. Bacchus was the legendary god of wine, and the name —"

"Aw!" grunted The Early Bird, entirely mollified. "I gotcha, boss; that was just a highbrow way, of sayin,' 'Let's wet the tonsils.' Sure, I'm on; but hereafter when you're gonna slip me an invite to a drink, it ain't necessary to be so dang fancy about it." With alacrity he touched the gong which summoned Nogo, Mr. Clackworthy's Japanese servant. James and Nogo had a sort of private code between them, and he struck four measured strokes, the signal that liquor, ice, and Seltzer were to be brought. Obedient to the summons, the smiling little Jap came in a few minutes later with a tray containing the requisite ingredients for high balls. Also he brought, tucked under his arm, the afternoon edition of the Chicago newspapers. There were four, for Mr. Clackworthy took them all and read them, from first pages to last; not even did he skip the want ads. It was not infrequently that he garnered from a chance item a bit of valuable information for his "prospect list," or even the nucleus of an idea that, under the chemistry of his mental processes, could be turned to handsome profit.

After sipping his high ball, the master confidence man picked up his newspapers and began a brief but nonetheless thorough survey of the printed columns. For almost an hour he was so occupied, when he reached page three of *The News*, the last of the daily publications to reach his attention. Without any comment to The Early Bird who, from the chair by the window was watching eagerly for any signs of a captured idea that might launch them upon a fresh adventure, Mr. Clackworthy put clown the paper and lighted a fresh cigar.

Silently, absently, he smoked, meditatively and without haste; his eyelids slightly lowered; now and then he touched his long, shapely fingers to the close-cropped Vandyke beard. Presently, he stirred and reached for the decanter to mix himself another high ball.

"Join me, James, and drink to the success of our latest pilgrimage in the quest of some yet unknown but carelessly tended surplus of this world's goods," he invited.

"Whatcha mean, boss?" demanded The Early Bird. "Ain'tcha got the goof picked out and numbered yet?"

"To speak in the metaphor of the shearer, my dear James," answered Mr. Clackworthy with a laugh, "we have, I think, a sharp pair of shears, but there yet remains to be found — the lamb. However, since we have the assurance of that high authority, Mr. P. T. Barnum, now deceased, that one is born every minute, I think we need entertain no fears on that score."

"Spill it!"

But the master confidence man kept his own counsel as he proceeded, between sips of his second drink, to work out various details of his yet rather embryonic scheme. After some minutes he again glanced at the third page of *The News* and then, stepping to a bookcase, he took down an atlas of the world. He turned to the map of Pennsylvania and, as The Early Bird watched him in a mounting fever of curiosity, gave studied attention to it.

"Adventure!" remarked Mr. Clackworthy. "The pot of gold at the end of the rainbow! Captain Kidd's treasure chest of pirated booty buried beneath ten feet of sand on the deserted isle! Capital!"

"Them two high balls has skyrocketed to your head, ain't they?" demanded The Early Bird with considerable asperity. "Hanged if that chin music don't sound like you was goin' in for this free verse stuff. Ain't no sense to that lingo you're spielin'. Cut out the verbal ring-around-the-rosy an' get down to biz."

Mr. Clackworthy took a gold pencil from his vest-pocket and pressed the point of it against the dot which the Pennsylvania map makers had labeled "ALSCHOOLA" and which, from the capitals, it could be judged was a county seat. Reference to the population list, alphabetically arranged in the back of the atlas, told him that Alschoola had been censused at ten thousand souls.

"If you want to make yourself useful, James," he said, "you might start packing. We go to Alschoola, Pennsylvania, tonight; to be more exact, we start tonight. Seeing that it is some distance from the route of the through New York trains, I hazard the guess that we will arrive about day after tomorrow."

The Early Bird blinked.

"Is that on the level, boss?" he demanded. "Are we grabbin' a rattler for this burg that is pronounced with a sneeze?"

"Never more serious in my life," affirmed Mr. Clackworthy. It was to be seen that he was generating a high-voltaged enthusiasm for this new scheme, whatever it might be.

"Play the record, boss; lemme in on the know."

Mr. Clackworthy shook his head teasingly; it always amused him to see The Early Bird tortured on the rack of curiosity.

"Perhaps our liquid refreshment, James, sharpened my wits a bit; but on page three of yonder paper you will find our lead. Suppose you look it over and tell me what you think of it."

The other leaped from his chair and grabbed the copy of *The News*, but in vain did his eyes sweep up and down the columns from left to right and from right to left again. He remained as puzzled as before. True enough, there were several Associated Press dispatches from Pennsylvania, but he found none of them mentioning the town with the queer-sounding name of Alschoola. In Philadelphia, a judge had suffered a nervous breakdown as a result of trying more than a thousand divorce cases; in Pittsburgh a kidnapped boy had been returned to his broken-hearted parents.

With an impatient growl, The Early Bird threw down the paper and turned on his heel.

"Watcha goin' to this here Alschoola for?" he demanded flatly.

"Money," answered Mr. Clackworthy with unilluminating brevity.

II.

James Early did not find his first glimpse of Alschoola reassuring. As he and the master confidence man disembarked from a non-Pullman train, the only kind that operated over the twenty-five-mile branch, his first impression was that the railroad company did not care enough about Alschoola to bestow upon it a respectable passenger station. Away from the shabby depot there extended a bumpy cobblestone street, leading uphill toward the business section.

The Early Bird wasn't wildly enthusiastic about the business part of the town, either. Accusingly he swung upon the master confidence man and glared.

"I hope you ain't got no idear that we're gonna take any dough outta this place?" he demanded with disgusted skepticism. "Huh! The whole burg wouldn't auction off for fifty berries — of my jack."

"Appearances," reminded Mr. Clackworthy, "are often deceiving. And permit me to say that a town is but the composite of its strongest personalities, now and then of but one dominating personality; towns, like the men who make them, have traits of individuality. What strikes you, on the surface, as being Alschoola's outstanding trait?"

"Freezin' onto the jack," snapped The Early Bird promptly; "squeezin' down on the silver dollar until the eagle squawks an' Lady Columbia sobs for mercy."

"Right!" and Mr. Clackworthy nodded. "Step to the head of the class." He gestured toward the shabby buildings and the poorly paved, ill-lighted street ahead of them. "Here we see a miserly municipal spirit and a horror of high taxes. I think it would be a safe guess to say that Alschoola is dominated by a clique of dollar-worshiping gentlemen who find progress too expensive for their tastes. Such men, my dear James, are the sort we like to pluck."

The Early Bird grunted without enthusiasm; for himself, he preferred to have some visible evidence of the wealth that they proposed to gather in.

"When I was liftin' leathers," he said, referring to those days previous to his association with the master confidence man, "I never picked out no panhandlers when the fins was itchin' for a fat roll."

There was no station bus, the lack of a public conveyance being explained by the proximity of the hotel sign, "Alschoola House," prominently displayed half a block up the dingy street. There being, likewise, no hotel porter to lighten their burden, the two plotters had no choice but to pick up their bags and make their way hotelward.

On the corner, before reaching the hostelry, they had to pass a rusty-looking building with peely lettering on the plate-glass window which announced: "Alschoola State Bank." Crowded up against the window was a desk before which sat a man who at the moment was fondling a packet of currency.

"See the money buzzard!" remarked The Early Bird.

Mr. Clackworthy smiled; he had to admit that there was something about the man at the bank desk, onion-smooth of pate, narrow-eyed, and with a beaked nose curving down over the upper lips of his thin mouth, which did make one think of a bird of prey.

"I wonder if that is the chief mogul of Alschoola," he said. "What a joy it would be to separate him from some of the money which he strokes so fondly!"

"Yeah," snorted The Early Bird, "an' what a joy it would be to breeze into the subtreasury some quiet P.M., an' stroll leisurely forth with a coupla suit cases full of thousand-case notes. It would be easier to take two or three million outta the mint than to bilk that bozo outta two bits."

The Alschoola House extended no cordial hand of welcome. The lazy-eyed, slow-moving clerk was smoking a corn-cob pipe as he watched two bearded oldsters engrossed with a game of checkers. Almost reluctantly, he tore himself away to receive the two incoming guests from Chicago.

Casting a further disapproving glance over the lobby, The Early Bird waited for Mr. Clackworthy to register. The lobby was shabbily and indifferently furnished with cane-bottomed chairs, numerous cuspidors, and a long, battered table for traveling salesmen to write their letters, at present given over to the checker game. The hotel desk itself was a counter, the top of which was covered with carpeting; at the end of it stood a fly-speckled cigar case of very doubtful-looking smokes.

"Two rooms with baths," murmured Mr. Clackworthy mechanically as he affixed his name and that of James Early to the untidy register. It was the order that he always gave for accommodations.

"Huh?" A surprised ejaculation came from the shirt-sleeved clerk, and he stared sharply, suspecting that he was being made the butt of banter.

"Two rooms and baths, if you don't mind."

"How'll a shower do?" and the clerk snickered. "Josh Duncan's rheumatism says rain, an' the roof of No. 18 is some leaky."

"Ain'tcha got no bathtubs in this joint?" demanded The Early Bird indignantly.

The clerk, perceiving that the request for baths had been quite serious, ceased grinning. He suddenly realized that Alschoola House was entertaining two guests accustomed to luxury and willing to pay for it.

"Sorry, gentlemen," he said, "but we ain't got but one bath to the floor."

Mr. Clackworthy smiled philosophically, and even offered the clerk a cigar. Past experience had shown him that considerable information of value is often to be obtained from friendly knights of the hotel desk.

"Do the best you can for us," he said cheerfully. "We shall probably be here for some time." At this prospect The Early Bird gave voice to a mournful groan and sank miserably into a chair.

The clerk was now looking the pair over in a critically appraising survey, noting the faultless tailoring of Mr. Clackworthy's one hundred-and-fifty-dollar suit, the neat cut of his Vandyke beard, the expansive opulence which exuded from his tall, impressive figure.

"You ain't — hum — sellin' stock?" he ventured suspiciously.

"No."

"It wouldn't' be none of my put-in, nohow; only, if you was, I was goin' to tell you that the same train you come in on goes back in fifty minutes. This ain't no town for stock salesmen. Flint Whitecotton don't like nobody comin' in here an' packin' away Alschoola money — and what Flint Whitecotton says in this man's town, goes."

"Ah!" murmured Mr. Clackworthy, his eyes lighting with interest. "Quite the local nabob, Mr. Whitecotton."

"Yep! Owns half the town, an he's got a mortgage on the other half."

"Tell me," requested Mr. Clackworthy, "is he somewhat bald of head, with a hook-nose, and —"

"That's him, mister."

"I saw him as I passed the bank."

"Uh-huh; president of the bank. Owns the big store, flour mill, lumber yard, and —"

"An' the hotel, of course," chimed in The Early Bird from his slouched position in the chair.

"No, but I guess he will," and the clerk sighed. "He's got a mortgage on it. Like as not I'll lose my job then; we don't get along very well, Flint Whitecotton an' me. That's why I tipped you off in case you was sellin' stock. Old Flint got the city council to pass an ordinance taxin' every stock salesman a hundred dollars." He frowned, frankly puzzled; swiftly, he began checking over the list of possible businesses that might have brought the prosperous-looking gentlemen to Alschoola. Not groceries, farm implements, washing machines, patent churns — and certainly they were not book agents.

"I am an emissary of — progress," said the master confidence man.

The clerk blinked solemnly for a moment, then pounded his fist down on the carpeted top of the desk.

"You're a capitalist!" he exclaimed.

"Yes, I have been so accused."

"I ought to have guessed that right off, Mr. —" He gave a quick glance toward the register. "Mr. Clackworthy. I wonder now if you mebbe come to have a look at Whitecotton's twenty-acre tract east of town?" His tired, dreamy-looking eyes were alight now, and his voice trembled with eagerness.

Mr. Clackworthy shook his head and stated that such was not the case, but adding that he might be interested if the Whitecotton tract showed any opportunity of profit.

"It does!" the clerk cried. "There's a gold mine out there in the Whitecotton tract. If you're a capitalist, you're the man I want to talk to. There's a fortune in that deposit for them that puts it on the market. It won't take much capital."

"What sort of a deposit?"

"Statuary clay, that's what. My name's Lemuel Budkins, and you an' me ought to get together, for" — his voice raised triumphantly — "I got an option on that twenty acres of land."

It cannot be truthfully said that a deposit of sculptor's modeling clay appealed to Mr. Clackworthy as offering promise of much profit, but it did occur to him that this might, in some way or another, provide the wedge which would pry open the way into Flint Whitecotton's hoard.

"When you can spare a little time, Mr. Budkins," he said, "I'll be glad to talk things over."

"I got time right now," answered Budkins promptly; "that's all I have got." He grabbed two of the traveling bags and led the way up the hotel stairs.

A few minutes later, his forehead glistening with moisture, his eyes gleaming with the rebirth of dying hopes, he leaned forward in a chair, facing Mr. Clackworthy and The Early Bird, trying to convince them that he held the key to sudden and certain wealth.

"You see," said Mr. Budkins, "I got the idee from a feller what was boardin' down here last summer at my Aunt Mandy's. He ran across that clay deposit just by accident. Said it was the best statuary clay he ever seen. Him not havin' any capital, he let me in on it, so we organized a little company, and —"

"How much capitalization?" inquired Mr. Clackworthy.

"Oh, we ain't incorporated yet," replied Budkins. "Seems like De Vine — that's my partner's name — must have hit a snag or mebbe died or something for I ain't heard from him in most a year. I had two or three nice, encouragin' letters, an' then he quit writin' all of a sudden, but —"

"How far did you get with your promotion plans?" inquired the master confidence man.

"Not far, an' somethin' has got to be done quick, I took an option on Flint Whitecotton's twenty acres, an' it runs out on the first of the month. That's next Friday. Only paid him a hundred dollars for it, but" — he colored in embarrassment — "the truth is, Mr. Clackworthy, I ain't got any more money to pay for another option. You see, I let De Vine have four hundred dollars for his expenses, an' —"

"I gotcha," interrupted The Early Bird. "You been nicked for four hundred iron men."

Mr. Budkins looked puzzled for a moment and then flushed guiltily.

"I — I sort of begun to have that suspicion," he admitted haltingly.

"It ain't no suspicion; it's a lead-pipe cinch," said James. "Consider yourself an enrolled scholar in the School of Experience, an' a fully initiated member of The Ancient Order of Trimmed Mutts. You been buncoed, bilked, fleeced, flimflammed an' otherwise deprived of four hundred berries."

"My dear James!" reproved Mr. Clackworthy sternly. He turned apologetically to Budkins. "Have you tried to interest — ah — local capital?" he inquired politely.

"There ain't no local capital, except what Flint Whitecotton has got squeezed in them two graspin' fists of his," Budkins answered bitterly. "He ain't got no vision; can't see no further than a dollar can cast a shadow. I tried to get him interested, but he just laughed at me. I tell you, Mr. Clackworthy, it's a gold mine. Just think — thirty-five dollars a ton just for clay that can be dug off the top of the ground with a shovel. Just think of it! Easier than minin' coal, an' coal sellin' for about six dollars to the ton!"

Mr. Clackworthy could have reminded him that the consumption of sculptor's clay would total very few tons a year, that it was but an empty daydream. This, in fact, he proceeded to do, as gently and as kindly as possible.

"While I am quite certain, Mr. Budkins, that your deposit of sculptor's clay lacks financial possibilities, I feel almost certain that I can return you the money which you would otherwise lose in the venture, and perhaps some interest besides. I shall let you know this afternoon."

Lemuel Budkins' face mirrored both disappointment and relief; it is hard, sometimes, to surrender a daydream, but five hundred dollars is a great deal of money to a man who hasn't any. In the case of the hotel clerk, the capital which had been swallowed up in his foolish, visionary scheme represented frugal economies.

When Budkins had departed, The Early Bird let his gaze wander from the cracked washbasin and pitcher on the rickety washstand in the corner of the room, to rest disgustedly on Mr. Clackworthy's face.

"Say!" he exploded. "What's the grand idear? Are we goin' around the country weedin' back some other guy's graft, or are we out to grab a little kale on our own hook?"

Mr. Clackworthy looked thoughtful for a moment.

"James," he said slowly, "during our association, have I ever taken money from a poor man? Have I ever trimmed an honest man? In my own defense, I answer, 'No!' Every man who has contributed to us, has fallen victim to his own avarice.

"The idea, my dear James, is to build a neat little trap for the local Midas known as Flint Whitecotton; a man, if my surmise is correct, as hard as his front name. The idea, my indignant partner in crime, is to convince Banker Whitecotton that he had a grievous financial mistake in optioning that twenty-acre tract of his on the edge of town."

"An' sell the option back to him, huh? What's the lay? You ain't flirtin' with the idear that you're gonna make him fall for no sculptor's clay racket?"

"Hardly!" Mr. Clackworthy laughed. "Hardly that, I fear that our hard-headed, tight-fisted banker is not so credulous as Mr. Burkin. Bestir yourself, and we shall have a look at that twenty acres of clay land."

The tract was but three miles from town, and thirty minutes later the two pursuers of easy money had made the trip in a hired flivver and were looking over the property. It was, indeed, as worthless-looking a piece of real estate as one might expect to find in the entire State of Pennsylvania. Half of it was a tangle of starved underbrush, and the remaining part of it was devoid of any growing thing, for the whitish clay was lacking in fertility. In the hot sun it was baked brick hard.

For a quarter of an hour Mr. Clackworthy devoted himself to a survey of the property, his brows knitted in thought. He noticed particularly that the State highway ran alongside the twenty acres. Although he nodded, The Early Bird's wrath grew apace.

"And now," said the master confidence man, "we will go back and proceed to take Mr. Whitecotton's measure."

"His name may be cotton," grunted James, "but I'll lay a li'le bet that you ain't gonna pick him."

"That's a sporting proposition. Any amount you like."

"A hundred seeds, boss." He cast a last disgusted glance at the desolate twenty acres and shook his head. It didn't seem humanly possible that any sane man would give up good money for it; he thought of the mysterious news item which had inspired the idea — and wondered with a curiosity which burned almost to fever heat.

III.

The building which housed the Alschoola State Bank gave no outward appearance of opulence, and neither did Mr. Flint Whitecotton, the bank's president. He wore a suit even more shabby than was the building; one judged his favorite axiom to be "A penny saved is a penny earned." The suit was frayed, threadbare, and darned in several places. The cuffs of his shirt wore aged whiskers; his shoes were unshined, as if he begrudged the cost of the polish necessary to give them a gloss; even the smoothness of his head was an item of economy. It did away with the necessity of barber bills.

Flint Whitecotton had a leathery skin, drawn drum tight over his bones. His eyes held a cold, freezing quality, and, as the bank door opened that afternoon, he frowned in black disfavor at the sinful extravagance as represented by Mr. Amos Clackworthy's perfect harmony of attire. Such sartorial prodigality, in the opinion of Mr. Whitecotton, was downright criminal.

Wasting no time in the little pleasantries generally attending a formal introduction, Mr. Clackworthy opened his wallet and put in front of the banker five bills, each of one thousand dollars' denomination. Mr. Whitecotton's eyes bulged.

"I wish to open an account," said the master confidence man crisply. "My name is Clackworthy, my home Chicago. If you desire business references —" He knew there would not be a call for them, although he could readily have supplied them; a five-thousand-dollar cash deposit speaks for itself. Worshipfully, the banker's fingers went out and began to stroke the beloved thousand-dollar bills. He gave the new depositor a look of baffled curiosity.

"Humph!" he grunted. His voice was like his face — harsh and unpleasant. "May I ask if you contemplate — ah — going into business here?"

"You might call it that."

"What line?"

"I propose to develop a resource that has been locally overlooked." Mr. Clackworthy smiled as he spoke. "If you will kindly give me credit for the five thousand, and a check book, I will write to your order a check for two thousand dollars."

"Huh? Check — two thousand — to my order?" gasped Mr. Whitecotton. He again stared at the new customer, this time as if searching for some outward signs of insanity.

"Precisely. You see, I have purchased from Lemuel Bodkins his option on that twenty acres of clay land east of town, and I wish to exercise the option. The check, if you please. You'll pardon me if I seem rather abrupt, but there are so many things I want to attend to — lumber for the buildings, some telegrams, and that sort of thing. Quite a lot of detail to getting a new enterprise started, you know."

As the banker mechanically made a notation in a pass book, an ill-concealed sneer twisted his thin lips.

"You are buying that clay land?" he demanded incredulously.

"Quite so." Already Mr. Clackworthy had uncapped his fountain pen and was filling in a check. "Just give me a receipt for it, and you can make the deed out later; tomorrow will do."

"What are you going to do with it?" demanded the banker bluntly.

"Extract a certain chemical property valuable to science,"

replied the confidence man glibly; and then, with a laugh: "Oh, I assure you that it has nothing to do with sculptor's clay, Mr. Whitecotton. You would hardly expect me to be wasting my time with an insignificant scheme like Budkins'. The poor chap has had his little dream and, fortunately, gets out with a whole skin and a little to spare. I gave him seven hundred dollars for his option."

"What?" The banker's tone rose to a shrill note for two reasons. One was because it seemed such an unnecessary waste of money — seven hundred dollars tossed away to a visionary young fool like Lem Budkins, when a hundred would have done quite as well; the other was that the option would have expired within another week. This extravagantly dressed stranger evidently wanted the twenty acres badly, and how Flint Whitecotton would have made him pay!

"Sure," said Mr. Clackworthy. "I felt sorry for the chap." The banker shivered; such costly pity was beyond his ken. Immediately he formed a very low regard for Mr. Clackworthy's ability as a business man.

IV.

Within the succeeding days, Alschoola was shown some speed. A neat but inexpensive shack went up on the Whitecotton twenty acres, almost overnight. Mr. Clackworthy paid spot cash for the lumber and the carpenter hire. The town, of course, was abuzz with speculation and guesses; but no one except Mr. Clackworthy knew, and he didn't tell. Even The Early Bird was not, as he would say, "in on the know," a fact which galled him bitterly.

With the completing of the shack and a high board fence, total cost eight hundred dollars, the two mysterious strangers began to keep regular hours, admitting no one. The town wondered what they did there, and would have been further mystified to have witnessed the strange capitalist calmly stretched out in a steamer chair, reading a volume of Freud's *Psychoanalysis*, while The Early Bird paced the floor like a caged lion, smoking countless cigarettes and muttering angrily.

It was midafternoon and James gave way to his daily explosion.

"I gotta have a look-in!" he stormed. "You gotta tell me what the lay is."

Mr. Clackworthy looked up lazily.

"We are going to sell Mr. Whitecotton's worthless farm back to him — at a handsome profit," he answered innocently. "I thought you knew that."

"But how are you gonna hook him?" demanded The Early Bird. "What's the bait we're usin'?"

"Gold," answered Mr. Clackworthy solemnly, "a pot of gold. Didn't you read that item on the third page of —"

"I didn't see nothin' from no Pennsylvania towns except —"

"As it happens," interrupted Mr. Clackworthy with a chuckle, "it wasn't a news item from any Pennsylvania town, but an Associated Press dispatch from Washington, D. C., relating to a certain Congressional inquiry which is now in progress and occupying generous amounts of space almost daily. Question me no further, James; this is a little guessing contest of mine. Try your luck at it."

"You know I ain't got a chance."

"Very well, I'll add a bit more," said Mr. Clackworthy, "Our mutual friend and often able assistant, George Bascom, will arrive in Alschoola day after tomorrow. He will remain entire stranger to both of us. We've never seen him before; we don't know him from Adam's off-ox.

"George will appear in Alschoola garbed in tatters which will make a Russian refugee look like Beau Brummel. He is empty of pocket and desperate of mind; he appeals to Banker Whitecotton. Mr. Whitecotton is skeptical and at the same time credulous. He doesn't believe George's story, but it has such a ring of truth, backed up by such a wealth of newspaper accounts, that he dare not ignore the chance of finding out if it is really true that his clay land is worth, not a mere two thousand dollars, but a hundred times that sum."

"Two hundred thousand smackers?" gasped The Early Bird.

"Your multiplication is correct," and Mr. Clackworthy nodded. "Mr. Whitecotton will be half convinced that his clay farm is worth two hundred thousand dollars in cash. And, on the evening of the day after tomorrow, George will proceed to convince him entirely — by a personally conducted visit to this very spot. Does it now become clear to you, my dear James?"

"Huh! Just as clear, boss, as a cloudy day on Lake Mich," The Early Bird remarked, then groaned. "Come on an' gimme a look-in."

Mr. Clackworthy shook his head teasingly and glanced at his watch.

"Come to think about it," he murmured, "I'll have to be getting to the bank for a little talk with Mr. Whitecotton. He's got a sight draft on me for thirty-two hundred dollars, and I've only eighteen hundred on deposit to meet it."

"Whatcha talkin' about? Ain'tcha got five thousand iron men in your kick?"

"True enough," said the master confidence man, "but what is in my pocket is not for Mr. Whitecotton to know. He is to be only aware that of the five thousand dollars I deposited in his bank, just one thousand eight hundred dollars remain. And — I don't want to meet the draft, anyhow. It's one that Pop Blanchard sent here; just a little touch in realism."

Half an hour later, Mr. Clackworthy, not looking so cheerful as he inwardly felt, was closeted with the local banker. Almost accusingly, Mr. Whitecotton produced the sight draft, a demand that one Mr. Amos Clackworthy pay over the sum of three thousand two hundred dollars forthwith.

"What about this?" he demanded.

"It's for some machinery that I have ordered, and which won't be shipped until it is paid," said Mr. Clackworthy with apparent glumness. "I need that machinery, and I need it bad. I can't get started until I have it; things haven't gone as smoothly as I had anticipated, and I hope that you —"

"There is but one question before me," cut in the banker icily. "Have you the money to meet this draft, or shall I sent it back unpaid?"

"You've got to help me out, Mr. Whitecotton," pleaded Mr. Clackworthy, "I've got a balance of one thousand eight hundred dollars on deposit; I need one thousand four hundred dollars to meet the draft. I paid you two thousand dollars for the land; suppose you lend me one thousand four hundred dollars on a ten-day note, with the land as security."

Banker Whitecotton laughed shrilly.

"Lend you one thousand four hundred dollars on that pile of clay?" he snorted. "It isn't worth fifty dollars an acre. I wouldn't give you thirty dollars an acre for it."

"But I paid you a hundred an acre."

"A bargain is a bargain," retorted the banker. "No one asked you to buy that land from me. Don't argue; I won't lend you a dollar on your hare-brained scheme."

"That's because you don't understand the chemical possibilities," persisted Mr. Clackworthy with just as much earnestness as if he had really expected to win the man over. He launched into a long, apparently technical, explanation of his contemplated process of extracting certain expensive chemicals from that peculiar whitish loam — all of which was Greek to the Alschoola banker.

"See here, Mr. Whitecotton," he went on, "I stand on the brink of success or failure. There has been a slight hitch in my plans; the money I expect to get has not come into my hands yet. I hope —"

"So did half-witted Lem Budkins," snapped Whitecotton.

"Take a look at this," pleaded Mr. Clackworthy, producing a letter. It was ostensibly from a New York chemical company offering him twenty thousand dollars for his entire rights. The banker, of course, had no way of knowing that those letterheads had been printed on Mr. Clackworthy's order and mailed by Pop Blanchard in New York; nevertheless, he tossed it aside with hardly a glance.

"Not interested," he said harshly. "You haven't the money to pay the draft; therefore, I send it back."

"And force me to sell out for a paltry twenty thousand dollars!" Mr. Clackworthy exclaimed bitterly. Mr. Whitecotton winced; it hurt him to hear such a sum sneeringly referred to as "paltry."

V.

The following afternoon, on the five o'clock train, George Bascom arrived in Alschoola. According to previous instructions, he was shabbily dressed, wore a dented derby hat, and had a four-day bristle of beard on his normally round and clean-shaven face.

He slouched almost furtively up the street away from the railroad station. The bank, of course, was closed, but he made inquiries at Hope's Drug Store and had himself directed to the residence of Flint Whitecotton. The banker was on the front porch of his cottage — it, like everything else he owned, had been secured with the smallest possible outlay of cash — fanning himself with a palm-leaf fan, which was an advertisement and had cost him nothing, waiting for supper. He glared at the approach of the ragged stranger.

"Go away!" he called. "We don't feed tramps."

"Mr. Whitecotton," said George. "I'm no tramp, and you've got to listen to me. I'm a chauffeur, and —"

"Save your breath; I don't need a chauffeur. I haven't any automobile — not with gasoline at thirty cents a gallon. Sinful extravagance, that is!"

"I don't want a job, either," went on George Bascom; "I don't want money or free food or a job. All I want is that you should listen to me."

"Well, so long as it don't cost anything," agreed Banker Whitecotton a little less grudgingly, "I'll listen."

"To keep you from throwing me off the place for a lunatic," began George, "I'll show you some of these newspaper clippings." He poked a grimy hand into his pocket and brought out a half dozen badly worn newspaper clippings. "Just glance over those, and then I'll talk."

Flint Whitecotton did glance them over, and his impatience gave way to curiosity.

"Well?" he demanded.

"Maybe you wonder why I come to you," went on George. "I'll tell you why. It's because I'm too dead broke to buy so much as a shovel to dig for the gold that is buried — I won't tell you where until we make a deal. Any minute I'm liable to be arrested as a vagrant. Your city marshal followed me three blocks when I got off the train. Two hundred thousand dollars in gold weighs a lot more than anyone man can pack. There's got to be a car to take it away. Understand? I've got to have help. Sure, I might have gone in with some crook, but he'd probably have knifed me in the back for my share.

"If I tell you where it's buried, do we split fifty-fifty? There's only two people on earth who know where it's hid, me and the woman, and she don't dare to make a move, on account of the government agents watching her so close. Do we make a deal?"

There was a light of fascination in Flint Whitecotton's cold, blue eyes; as Mr. Clackworthy had predicted, he could hardly believe it, and yet he dared not doubt it entirely. There was just one thing that decided him — no expense was involved.

"I'll go in with you," he agreed, "I'll buy the shovels. We don't have to go to the cost of hiring an automobile until we're sure it's where you say it was buried. Where is that place?"

"On your own land," answered George Bascom, "that patch of yours out on the State road. It's buried four feet down in the clay. I can take you right to the spot; I'll take you now."

A hoarse cry burst through the lips of the miserly banker. The land that he had sold for two thousand dollars was worth almost a quarter of a million dollars in buried treasure!

VI.

Even Mr. Clackworthy in his most confident moments had not anticipated that things would go through to such a whirlwind finish. He had not dreamed that the banker's greed would be so sharply whetted that he would plunge in, head over heels, within a few hours. The reason for it, no doubt, was Whitecotton's fear that George Bascom, to all appearances the penniless, desperate possessor of a two-hundred-thousand dollar secret, would discover that he, the banker, was no longer the owner of the treasure-bearing twenty acres. George, too, must have told his story well and convincingly for the cautious, canny miser to have swallowed it, hook, line, and sinker.

But that is just what happened, and Mr. Clackworthy, who had planned many further elaborate details, was totally unprepared to receive a summons from Flint Whitecotton the next morning.

"Mr. Clackworthy," began the banker, "perhaps I was — um — rather hasty with you during our last talk. However, I have — ah — been thinking it over, and I have decided that I owe it as my duty as a — ah — a public-spirited citizen to take an interest in this budding enterprise of yours. That letter you showed to me, in which you were offered twenty thousand dollars to sell out — that in itself shows that your venture must have merit."

Mr. Clackworthy looked discouraged.

"I was just on the verge of sending a wire to the New York firm, telling them that I would accept twenty-five thousand dollars and get out. They expected, of course, to raise the ante when they offered twenty thousand dollars. The truth of it is, Mr. Whitecotton, that I'm too small a fellow to fight the big combine; that's what scared off the capital that had been promised me. My hands are up; I quit. There's no use in talking things over; I'm going to sell out."

"I wouldn't do that," interposed Banker Whitecotton hastily. "Now why can't we form a company? Perhaps I would put up ten thousand dollars, but — um — I would, of course, expect to control."

"I'd rather sell out than be frozen out later," retorted Mr. Clackworthy shrewdly. "No, so long as I'm whipped, I'll take all the money I can get." He started to get from his chair, but the banker stopped him insistently. They talked for two long, haggling hours, and at length, cold sweat pouring from his bald forehead, Flint Whitecotton, the stingiest man whom Amos Clackworthy had ever done business with, inclined his head slowly, reluctantly; he agreed to give twenty-five thousand dollars.

Again Mr. Clackworthy and The Early Bird were passengers on the non-Pullman train on the branch line which terminated at Alschoola. This time, however, they were bound away from the shabby, unprogressive town, for which James was thankful; within the wallet of the master confidence man reposed twenty-five thousand dollars in currency, and for this they were both thankful.

But The Early Bird's forehead was corrugated with a puzzled frown.

"I ain't got it all through the old bean yet, boss," he admitted. "You're tryin' to tell me that the old dollar squeezer come across with twenty-five thousand smackers because he swallowed George Bascom's fairy tale about there bein' a coupla hundred thousand in the yellow stuff in the terra firma of that clay farm you bought off'n him for a coupla thousand berries?"

"It was realism, that did the trick, my dear James," said Mr. Clackworthy, chuckling. "That, and his naturally greedy, grasping nature. Moreover, he thought he was playing safe so far as his twenty-five thousand is concerned. Before he closed with me, he sent a wire to The Gotham Chemical Corporation, asking them if they would give twenty-five thousand dollars to buy me out; since The Gotham Chemical Corporation is Pop Blanchard, the answer was 'Yes.' He didn't suspect a flimflam, because he couldn't imagine any sane man who would risk paying out two thousand dollars on a long chance."

"What I'm gettin' at, boss," said The Early Bird, "is, what was the hocus-pocus that made him fall for George Bascom's fake about that buried gold?"

"You're hopeless," and Mr. Clackworthy sighed. "You read the newspapers every day, too. Certainly you should recall that for some time there has been a Congressional inquiry regarding a certain war slacker named Grover Blindhouse, who escaped from army imprisonment and made his way to Europe. The Congressional inquiry brought out that the young man's mother, the widow of a wealthy Pennsylvania brewer, got together the astounding sum of two hundred thousand dollars in cash and buried it not many miles from Philadelphia for her son's use in his flight. However, the money is still buried; she dare not try to recover it, for fear that secret-service agents will shadow her and the government confiscate it, and she won't tell where it was buried. The clipping which gave me the inspiration for this very profitable adventure of ours —"

He paused and reached into his pocket. The Early Bird accepted the scrap of paper and read:

SEEK BLINDHOUSE CHAUFFEUR WHO DROVE $200,000 TREASURE CAR

*Congressional Inquiry Reveals Name of
Man Who Can Lead Way
to Buried Wealth.*

"I gotcha, boss!" exclaimed The Early Bird. "George Bascom slipped Whitecotton a yarn about bein' the missin' chauffeur."

"As a finishing touch," continued Mr. Clackworthy, "I've given the old miser something to puzzle about. At the spot where he will dig, there is planted an iron chest containing — a hundred dollars in pennies. And that's your money, by the way, James."

"But," said The Early Bird with an apprehensive shudder, "that bird is gonna be some wild — if he don't drop dead on the spot. What if he starts investigatin' an' find's that fake chemical company —"

"Checkmate!" exclaimed Mr. Clackworthy. "The only way he can get us convicted, my dear James, is to plead guilty himself to a conspiracy against the government. We have got him, as they say, going and coming."

YELLOW ELEPHANTS
by Harold Lamb

CHAPTER I.
A YOUNG MAN IN A HURRY.

The watch of Andrew Hollis told him that he had sixteen minutes to catch his train. His memory told him he had forgotten something. Instinctively he slowed his steps and ransacked his mind for the missing item.

His bag? No, he had that well stocked with traveling kit and necessary clothing. Pullman reservation — money? His tickets were in his coat-pocket, likewise an unopened week's pay-envelope. Had he left anything at the office?

Andrew Hollis was a methodical young man, and he was sure that he had closed and locked his desk in the Wall Street office of the News' financial page upon nothing that did not belong there when he left that afternoon bound for New England and Aunt Emma!

"Aunt Emma!" he thought swiftly. "Great guns — I haven't any present for her!"

For seven years, ever since his start in business in New York, Andrew Hollis had been accustomed to pay a three-days' visit to Aunt Emma Hollis, his nearest living relative. And he had never neglected to bring some gift, as it was Mrs. Hollis's birthday.

He glanced hurriedly around. He was in the thick of the crowd at Fifth Avenue and Forty-Third Street. Beside him a shop window caught his eye, with its sign:

WONG LI
Oriental Art

The window contained a costly Samurai vase and an elaborate silken mandarin's robe. Rather high-priced stuff, he thought, but Aunt Emma was fond of collecting Chinese trinkets.

Thus Hollis reasoned, and thereby exposed himself for three minutes to a whim of fate involving other lives.

He pushed hastily through the door. A Chinaman in a businesslike black suit bowed, with the courtesy of the Oriental salesman. Hollis sighted two ivory elephants standing on the counter beside an array of elaborate fans. They were grotesque beasts, a faded yellow in color, perhaps ten inches high, and resting on ebony stands. He picked up the nearest one.

"How much for this?" he asked hastily.

"Fourteen dollars and a half," stated the Oriental concisely.

The other elephant seemed to Hollis to be more faded in color; moreover, it was undeniably scratched. It might be cheaper, he reasoned.

"That one is very rare," the Chinaman responded to his question with a shake of the head, "it is fine ivory. It is old Ming work. A customer left it here to be sold. The price is four hundred dollars. The other is inferior ivory —"

"It's good enough for me," announced Hollis hastily. He set the Ming quadruped back on the counter and extracted his pay-envelope. From the bills inside it he took three five-dollar bills. Throwing the crumpled envelope on the floor, he handed the Chinaman the money, indicating the elephant he had first looked at. "Aunt Emma knows something about ivories, but she won't know that I know the difference — so it's a good risk."

The shopkeeper glanced shrewdly from Hollis to the animals and departed rearwards for the change, leaving the elephants on the counter. Absently, Hollis noted that he joined one of his countrymen, talking in a curtained recess at the back of the store. His customer jerked out his watch. The sixteen minutes had been reduced to seven. And it was a little more than two blocks to the Grand Central.

Hollis, by instinct and professional training, was accustomed to act expeditiously. Within ten seconds he had snapped open his suitcase, dropped into it the yellow elephant and ebony stand and gained the door. As he did so he heard an exclamation in the rear of the store and hurried steps coming toward him.

"Keep the change, John!" he cried, and was out in the street. He had a vague impression of loud voices issuing after him. Then he darted into the crowd.

The traffic at Forty-Second held him up for a precious minute. Dodging a bus and sliding past the traffic cop, he made the other side of Fifth Avenue with a precarious margin of safety. Seven years of financial statistics had not served to eradicate his New England country vigor, and a serviceable pair of legs, aided by a keen eye, enabled him to gain the upper level of the Grand Central and the vestibule of the Boston sleeper just before the porters hopped aboard the moving train. As it was, he was the last person but one to make the train.

Seating himself in his section with the gratification of the man who has bought his tickets in advance and defeated the combination of time-table and clock by a matter of seconds, Hollis stowed his overcoat and bag on the seat beside him. He noticed that the car was filled.

Not until then did it occur to him that he had thrust his

new purchase hastily into the bag, and that it might be well to pack it securely against danger of breakage. He lifted the suitcase to his knees, picked up the curio, oblivious of the inquisitive glances cast his way by fellow travelers, and inserted it neatly between some clothing in the bag. Years of handling stock and bond quotations had bred exactitude of habit in Hollis, until even his New England aunt admitted that he was "careful with his things."

Satisfied, he pushed the suitcase under the seat, begging the pardon of a rather striking-looking blond lady for disturbing her as he did so. It struck him that Mrs. Hollis had written him a note which he had only time to glance at hastily that day owing to the pressing need of clearing his desk before leaving the office. He took it out now and ran over it leisurely.

As usual, his aunt informed him that she would meet him with the car — said the snow was two feet deep — and that she had killed a choice turkey in honor of his coming.

In the postscript, the most important part of a woman's letter, she added that a cousin of his was visiting the farm. Ruth Carruthers had come from New Orleans, he read, a charming girl. She knew that he would like her.

"Trust a widowed aunt," he thought disgustedly, "to assemble all the family chickens in the coop. I've never seen this Carruthers girl, and I don't want to. Ten to one she wants to know all about the big city, how many fish are in the aquarium, who built the Washington Arch, and why the Woolworth Building doesn't fall into the subway —"

Hollis ran a slim hand through his sandy hair with something like a groan. A darky waiter, pursuing his swaying course through the car, reminded him that the diner was open; and the hasty movement of passengers after the waiter recalled the fact that he would have to hurry, if he expected to get a seat.

Thrusting the letter into the pocket of his overcoat, Hollis picked up his cap and sought the diner.

CHAPTER II.
SOMETHING FOR NOTHING.

Dinner and a pipe in the smoking-compartment did not wholly relieve Hollis's irritation at the news contained in his aunt's note. Aunt Emma, he told himself, was a good sport who kept a supply of his favorite brand of tobacco waiting for him, and who cooked absolutely the best mince pies and buckwheat cakes in the State of New Hampshire. Why did she have to go and spoil his three-days' vacation by inviting a woman cousin, whom he would be expected to amuse, or, worse, might expect to amuse him?

Southerners, as he remembered them, were addicted to telling continuous jokes, at which he was bound to laugh. A confirmed bachelor, Andrew Hollis disliked women generally, particularly young girls, who, he assured himself, were always either trying to make a slave of him or use him to make other slaves jealous.

He skipped through his evening paper disconsolately, glancing at the story of a two-days' old jewel robbery at the Charity Ball and his own column of Wall Street news. He glanced up with a scowl as the porter thrust his head through the curtains of the compartment.

"Which of you gentlemen," inquired the factotum of the Pullman, "has lower eight?"

"I have," Hollis's scowl deepened. "What's the idea?"

"Well," informed the porter apologetically, "I reckon you ain't got it now, boss."

Hollis snorted and reached for his wallet. "I'd like to know why not. I have the ticket here."

"Look here, boss. This is whut happened. I made up lower eight like you told me. Soon as it was made up a lady done got into it. I told her it was your berth, but she said to tell you she hadn't any herself, an' the cyar was full. There ain't an empty berth in the train. So if you don't mind sleepin' here — she's trying to open her big suitcase on lower eight this minute, boss —"

"I do mind!" grunted the newspaperman. "Ask the lady if she won't take the upper. Maybe the man who has the upper will bunk in with me."

The porter scratched his head.

"The puhson in upper eight is another lady, sir. And the one in your berth ain't the kind you can ask. She said to tell you thank you for the berth, but she cain't sleep in the smoker and you can."

Hollis sheltered himself behind his paper from the ironical glances of his companions in the compartment.

"All right." He gave in. "Bring my bag and overcoat in here."

Immersed in his heavy coat, with the bag stowed under the leather settee, Hollis prepared to make the best of his quarters. The other men had retired to their sections, with the exception of a Jap, who was studiously reading a guidebook at the other corner of the seat.

Hollis had guessed the man to be a student at one of the eastern colleges — the country was full of them — whether a Jap or a Chinaman, he could not judge. In the absence of a pigtail, one looked like the other to him. And the man on the other side of the bench was neatly clad in very modern garments.

The rocking of the train and the gloom of the compartment — he had switched off the main lights — soon drew Hollis's thoughts into a sleepy haze. He lapsed into the dreamless half-sleep of the Pullman traveler.

Cold and the renewed clicking of rails speeding underfoot aroused him slightly. His stiff body and numb hands told him that he had been asleep some hours, and he was about to change to a more comfortable position when his eyes flew wide open. The settee was in gloom, but in a gleam of light coming through the curtains from the passageway without he saw his companion squatted on the floor.

The Oriental was bending over an object on the floor of the compartment. The object was Hollis's suitcase, and as he watched the man snapped back the catch and opened it.

The newspaperman did not move, but his glance searched the other keenly. The Chinaman seemed to be studying something among the articles in the bag, and so far as Hollis could judge, his expression was one of keen satisfaction.

"If I can lend you anything," observed Hollis amiably, "say so. If not —"

Abruptly the Oriental closed the bag, and slid it hastily to its former position under the settee. He rose, with a quick glance at the man on the seat. Standing in the light the Oriental was clearly exposed to Hollis's gaze. Without attempting to reply, he ducked out of the compartment.

Hollis waited until the other's footsteps had died away in the direction of the vestibule. Then he switched on one of the lights and drew out his suitcase. Opening it, he ran his hand swiftly over its contents. When he had made a hasty, but thorough, inventory of what the bag contained, he sat back with a puzzled frown.

Apparently the Oriental person had been moved by predatory motives; certainly there could be no confusing Hollis's bag with the other's small satchel. Yet, so far as he could see, nothing had been disturbed.

True, he had not seen the other take anything from the suitcase. But why anyone should go to so much trouble, even risk, to look at a few shirts or pajamas and a toilet kit, was more than Hollis could fathom. There was the yellow elephant, of course —

He took out the animal in question and surveyed it speculatively. As has been said, Hollis had a keen sense of property ownership. The attempted burglary of the Oriental, if it was that, annoyed him. The unlucky incident of the woman appropriating his berth had been responsible for it, he told himself.

Hollis gave a thoughtful whistle as he replaced the elephant. He remembered that the porter had said the lady had been trying to open the big suitcase on lower eight. Now, he recalled quite clearly that his own piece of baggage had lain in that section while he was in the diner. It was one of Hollis's pet axioms that nothing happens without a cause. Could the lady of lower eight have been anxious to see the inside of the bag, as well as the Oriental?

He pressed the button at the side of the settee, and the sleepy porter poked his head through the curtains, shoebrush in hand.

"Look here, Jonathan," interrogated Hollis amiably, "what kind of a lady was the one who grabbed my berth?"

The slave of the sleeper cast a shrewd eye at his questioner and decided that he meant well.

"Well, sir," he meditated, "she wuz a powuhful strong-minded lady. She had blond hair and black eyes. But I cain't find her shoes, nohow."

Hollis thought of the handsome and rather dressy woman who had shared his seat early in the evening when he had inspected his purchase. He exhibited a silver dollar.

"Some of the people are getting up, Jonathan," he observed. "Suppose you look once more for the blond lady's shoes, and see if she is in the berth. I may have left something there, and I would like to look around without disturbing her — if she happens to be out of the berth."

Such occurrences are part of the routine of a Pullman. The Negro led Hollis to lower eight and felt through the curtains discreetly. His expression changed, and he opened the hangings. Peering over his shoulder, the newspaperman saw that the berth was empty. It had not been slept in, but the bedclothes were rumpled, as if someone had been sitting on them.

"She certainly did get into lower eight, sir," the darky mused.

"Well, she's not here now," Hollis pointed out. "Any chance of her leaving the train?"

The porter grinned suddenly.

"I know how it was now, sir. She must have been the lady what wuz taken off the train at New Haven. Yes, sir. That wuz it."

"Sick?"

"I reckon you didn't hear her when she wuz taken off. Two plain-clothes gentlemen from New York headquarters held the train while they went through it. They pinched a lady in this cyar, I saw them assist her out the vestibule. Yes, sir. She done yell out they weren't no gentlemen to pull her off the train without a warrant. But one of the plain-clothes cops, he said, he reckoned there'd be warrant enough for her in New York."

"Did you hear her name? Also, what kind of a bag did she have with her?"

"They called her Gladys, I think, sir. A small hand-satchel, boss."

Hollis returned to the smoking-room, washed and shaved, and resumed his place on the settee. Within him stirred the righteous indignation of the man who has had his belongings tampered with. The porter had seen the blond lady of lower eight and police notoriety carry a small satchel from the train. But she had tried to unlock his own suitcase, just before the porter had restored it to him in the smoking compartment. A mistake? Hardly. His belongings, he reflected, had become suddenly of interest to his fellow-travelers.

Hollis laughed, realizing that the thing was absurd. Except for some toilet things and clothing, there was only the yellow elephant in the bag. And why should anyone, woman or Oriental, want to steal a yellow elephant, price fourteen dollars and fifty cents? He had exhibited the elephant he had purchased in the Pullman. Either the woman or the Oriental might have seen it there. But why should they immediately covet it?

He wondered if the Oriental was known by his first name, also, to the police. Or if he knew the woman. In that case, the man had not seemed disturbed by her removal — had gone about calmly investigating Hollis's bag. Unnoticed by him, the train had slowed to a halt at one of the towns on the outskirts of Boston. Hollis jumped out of the smoker into the passageway. He stumbled through the sleeper, looking for the Chinaman. He did not want the man to leave the train before he could question him.

But the train was already in motion again. The newspaperman halted in one of the vestibules, staring out through the glass door. On the platform of the station he saw in the gray light of early morning his companion of the smoking compartment standing, satchel in hand. As their glances met the other turned quickly and walked back into the station.

CHAPTER III.
A PIECE OF NEWS.

"**M**y goodness! Andy Hollis, you look as if your food in the city didn't agree with you!"

Mrs. Emma Hollis surveyed her nephew from a pair of bright eyes — the only thing visible in a medley of fur coat, muffler, and cap — as he climbed into the runabout beside her.

"I expect it will, for the next few days," grinned the newspaperman, sniffing the keen air with its scent of burning pine appreciatively. His aunt started the car with a practiced hand over the packed snow of the road into the mountains.

"Yes, I guess it will," she said brightly. "Ruth was putting a pan of biscuits into the oven when I left. She says she's going to make you some real, Southern waffles which will go fine with our maple syrup."

Hollis grunted. It was bad enough to have a strange girl on the place without her trying to cook things which he would have to eat. He had slept little on the trail and his temper had suffered accordingly. When he had put the runabout in the barn he took his suitcase to the room that had always been his, being careful to avoid the kitchen of the farmhouse, whence came sounds of voices and clatter of dishes.

He halted on the threshold of the room with an exclamation of disgust. A girl coat and fur cap were on the bed. An array of mysterious articles was on a new lace cover upon the bureau. A subtle perfume assailed his senses, very different from the accustomed smell of camphor and linen that pervaded his room.

"Oh, Andy" — the voice of his am floated up to him — "I didn't tell you that Ruth had your room! You have the spare room with Uncle Henry's portrait."

Hollis picked up his bag and sought his unaccustomed quarters with a scowl which had not entirely worn off when he descended to the dining-room with the ivory elephant under his arm. He found Aunt Emma seated at the table with his new cousin. He felt himself the target for a pair of warm, brown eyes.

Ruth Carruthers, he told himself with relief, was not a pretty girl. Later, he was not so sure of this point. She was pale, with a mass of heavy, dark hair, a fine pair of eyes. She wore a simple waist with heavy skirt and a pair of stout outing shoes.

"Why, Andy Hollis?" cried his aunt. "Whatever have you got —"

"Your birthday present," he explained. "A Chinese curio, aunty. It's — it's an antique elephant."

With a swift motion the mistress of the house seized on the article.

"My goodness! It's a treasure, Andy. Why, look, Ruth, it's the finest ivory. And such carving. It must have cost a mint of money."

Hollis nodded with some embarrassment. Now that his aunt had estimated the value of the thing, he thought, he could not very well tell her that he had actually bought an imitation. Uncle Henry had been a merchant skipper in the Pacific, and had brought home a collection of trophies from the Orient. Hence Mrs. Hollis's discrimination. She placed the elephant on its stand and eyed it with profound satisfaction.

"Why, yes, the thing has some value," he admitted. "Coming up on the train a car-thief went through my bag after it."

"A thief!" Ruth's eyes widened.

"Yes," announced Hollis, not unconscious of the effect of his words on his cousin; "and also, perhaps, the woman who was in my berth."

Aunt Emma paused in the act of handing him a plate of

warm biscuits.

"In your berth?"

"Oh, I had to give it up to her!" Hollis hastened to add. "Just before some cops from the big town pulled her off at New Haven. Seems that she was wanted. These are fine biscuits, aunty."

"I'm so glad you like them, Mr. Hollis," his cousin smiled. "I was afraid to try to make them, but your aunt insisted."

"Oh, are they yours?" Hollis was surprised. He did not see the girl flush at his tone. He was afraid that she would come into the sitting room with him when he retired, as of hallowed custom, to smoke his pipe, with the morning paper. But Miss Carruthers vanished upstairs. He scanned the pages indifferently between puffs of Mrs. Hollis's excellent tobacco. Suddenly he sat up alertly.

The account of an accident in the maelstrom of New York business had caught his eye.

CHINESE ART DEALER SHOT.
Wong Li, Proprietor of Fifth Avenue Curio
Shop, Victim of Unknown
Marauder's Bullet.

After the manner of a newspaper story, the time, the place, and the motive of the shooting were prominently set forth. At five minutes of six, the evening before, pedestrians on Fifth Avenue had heard a shot in the Chinese shop at Forty-Third Street. Wong Li had been found lying on the floor with a bullet wound in his head. His condition was serious. No others were found in the shop. The wounded man would make no statement as to the identity of the assassin.

The police declared, the story concluded, a man with a suitcase had been seen to run from the door of the store. This man had vanished down Forty-Second Street. As usual, the police announced that they had a clue to the person in question.

Hollis let the paper fall with a low whistle. Five minutes to six was approximately the time he had left Wong Li's place. But the proprietor had been in sound health, to the best of his knowledge. The shooting must have been immediately after his departure.

But, by whom? Events had transpired swiftly, he thought, for not only had Wong Li fallen by another's bullet during those eventful few moments just before six o'clock yesterday, but the curio he purchased had become an object of interest to others.

Hollis told himself that trouble seemed to follow the elephant. He reflected with a grim smile that it was the same that now reposed on his aunt's immaculate what-not. The smile faded as he read over the incident of the vanishing man with the suitcase. The description tallied too well with his own.

Aunt Emma entered the room.

"Get your snow-shoes, Andy. They're in the attic," she said brightly. "Ruth is going for a tramp in the woods with hers. It will do you good."

"I prefer the house!" grunted Hollis. "You know girls bore me! Just because I come to visit you, Aunt Emma, I don't have to play tag with a schoolgirl cousin —"

"Ruth isn't a schoolgirl," corrected the woman briskly. "She's a splendid little thing. You have no right to be so rude to her. And you must get used to her, Andy," she added mischievously, "because we two lone women are going to visit New York, and we expect to be taken care of by the man of our family. We are going back with you, and you must take us to all the good, new shows, and all the sights."

"Good Lord!" groaned Hollis.

"And," continued Aunt Emma thoughtfully, "I think we will stay at your rooms. They are attractive and neat. You can go to a hotel for a while. You see, Ruth may take some course at Morningside College — she has a letter of introduction to Professor de Bacourt, the Orientologist, an acquaintance of her French relatives in New Orleans."

Hollis made a feeble protest, which his aunt instantly overruled, knowing his fondness for her. Her heart was set on it, she said decisively. And Ruth had never been in New York.

"I suppose she will want to ride in the rubberneck bus!" suggested Hollis miserably.

"Of course. And we'll see the Aquarium."

CHAPTER IV.
TWO — NOT ALWAYS COMPANY.

The next morning, when he came downstairs, after a good night's sleep, the newspaperman found his cousin from New Orleans studying the ivory elephant curiously. A glint of sunlight through window curtains glowed on the girl's mass of bronze hair, and a delicate flush showed in her cheeks.

Hollis felt disconcertingly that if she was not pretty there was something about her decidedly attractive. Moreover, he found her silence discomposing. She was not at all as he had imagined her.

Hollis went to the window and looked out at the snow-carpeted lawn. He was conscious that the girl's gaze was on his back, and he swung around, squaring his shoulders.

"How do you like the yellow elephant?" he asked defiantly, feeling his cheeks warm unexpectedly.

Ruth's fine eyes went impartially from him to the curio.

"I adore puzzles," she observed calmly, "and this is a splendid one."

"Puzzles?"

"Yes. Don't you know that Chinese curios have lots of secret cubbyholes and things? Why, Chinese invisible boxes are famous. I spend hours in working them out. Mrs. Hollis has some right cute ones in her collection. But your elephant is really delicious."

Hollis stepped to her side and took up the animal in question, tapping it tentatively.

"Do you mean to say, Miss Carruthers," he demanded, "that there is an — er — compartment in this beast that escapes the eye?"

"More than one, Mr. Hollis." Something like a dimple appeared at the corners of his cousin's mouth. "It took me ages to find them."

Vague suspicion flooded upon Hollis. He recalled the curiosity of the Oriental in the smoker. Was it possible that the elephant housed valuables which were known to others, but not to himself? He examined every inch of the ivory surface attentively. He shook it, tapped it again, turned it over — with no result. Apparently there was no blemish on its smooth surface. Certainly it sounded solid.

"You don't seem to know where to look, Mr. Hollis," said the girl in a curious tone. She accented the *mister* as if unaccustomed to formality.

Hollis scowled and renewed his search fruitlessly.

"The thing's solid," he announced finally. "No mistake about that."

"Yes and no. Didn't the dealer tell you about the hidden compartments when you bought it? It's such a costly thing, isn't it? — I should think he would have explained all about it?"

Intent on his search, Hollis did not note her quickened interest.

"Costly? No, I paid only fifteen dollars for it."

Her brows wrinkled in a pretty frown.

"Don't you think it was a great bargain, Mr. Hollis?"

"Well, it looked just like a Ming antique worth hundreds," he said bruskly.

His cousin looked up quickly and the frown disappeared.

"I don't think you're as good at Chinese puzzles as I am," she laughed.

Hollis shrugged his shoulders rather irritably. "This is one I'll leave to you and Aunt Emma. Maybe the Oriental thief of the train was fond of puzzles, too. I confess I am not interested in them."

"Aren't you, Mr. Hollis?" Ruth stared at the yellow elephant meditatively. "Because Aunt Emma says this is really precious. She was wondering how you could afford to buy it."

"If you are good at puzzles, Miss Carruthers —" Hollis assured himself that the girl's curiosity was annoying; already she seemed to hint that he had practiced a deception on his aunt — "suppose you tell me why anyone should go to the trouble to rob my bag for this fifteen-dollar near-beauty. Also, why Aunt Emma thinks this is the real thing in ivory, when it's imitation. And what you found in these invisible chambers."

By way of answer the girl took up the elephant. With a slender forefinger she pressed in one of the animal's jeweled eyes, then the other. Hollis heard a faint click. To his surprise one of the ivory feet came off at the girl's deft touch.

He saw that the break was cleverly concealed by lines in the carving. Not one but four of the elephant's feet separated from the legs. Turning the animal upon its back, his cousin triumphantly pointed out four hollow chambers lined with velvet in the legs. Her forefinger, inserted in the opening, went as far as the second joint.

"The body is solid," she explained. "I suspected that the feet came off like in the toy dogs filled with candy we used to buy when we were children. But it took me hours to find the springs in the eyes."

"Did you find anything in it?" Hollis demanded eagerly.

"I found all there was to find."

"Meaning —"

"Four secret compartments with velvet lining."

The girl's dark eyes met his frankly. Hollis felt suddenly impatient at his excitement. An elephant with hollow legs. Nothing extraordinary about that. Why should Miss Carruthers look at him so queerly? He had told her he knew nothing about the beast. Yet he read a challenge in her gaze.

"It's really quite a puzzle, Mr. Hollis," observed Ruth absently. "Did you see in the paper that Wong Li had been shot?"

In spite of himself he started. What could Miss Carruthers know about Wong Li? Or, rather, how could she connect the curio dealer with the ivory elephant?

The girl picked up the ebony stand by the elephant and turned it over with a half-smile. On the bottom Hollis saw a square paster bearing the legend: *Wong Li, Chinese Art*, with a cabalistic trademark.

"Well, what do you make out of the puzzle, Miss Carruthers?" he said resentfully. The girl behaved as if she had him on the witness-stand.

"Nothing," his cousin smiled, "but I'd love to work it

out, and I do think you're mean not to help me."

She left him with a rankling sense of injury. He had come to New Hampshire to have an enjoyable outing. Not, he assured himself, to be pestered by the curiosity of a New Orleans cousin. The clatter of dishes and the laughter of Ruth and his aunt in the kitchen did not tend to soothe him. He was doomed to play chaperon and guide-of-all-work for his cousin on his return to New York. She would even take his rooms. When Mrs. Hollis looked into the room he met her with a dark scowl.

"Ruth's gettin' on her things to go down to the village for some groceries, Andy," his aunt remarked. "I told her you'd take her down in the car. It'll be a fine chance for you two to get to know each other —" Hollis had a vision of a renewal of Miss Carruthers's cross-questioning, and got to his feet purposefully.

"You know, Aunt Emma," he declared, "I wanted to go for a hike in the woods with my gun this morning. Ruth doesn't need a chauffeur —"

"Why, Andy? Someone ought to go with her for company!"

"Company!" Hollis's irritation reached the bursting point. "Aunt Emma, I thought you were a good sport. Now I see that you're a matchmaker, like the other women. Ten to one you want me to be the goat and marry Ruth! Did I ever apply for the post of gentleman-companion to — to one of our poor relations?"

The phrase escaped him before he knew just what he had said. A startled change in his aunt's face silenced him. Too late, he was aware of Miss Carruthers standing in the doorway. The girl's head was high, and her cheeks were flushed.

"I don't want to spoil Mr. Hollis's outing, Aunt Emma," she said quietly. "I reckon I'll go to the village alone."

CHAPTER V.
FEATHERING A NEST.

Tom Lemoire, self-christened in this fashion for the time being, placed his gray doeskin and patent-leather-shod feet upon the near-mahogany of the center table in the Lemoire apartment on Riverside Drive and flicked the ash from his cigarette under a gilt chair.

"Gladys," he remarked in a cloud of smoke, "as a sister, you're a gold-edge investment on the installment plan; but as a getaway artist, you class with last year's song-hit — you aren't there!"

A blond young woman of ample figure, with more than a suspicion of makeup around the eyes, stared at him sardonically.

"The other way around, Tom," she smiled indifferently, "I'm here. How was I to know the plain-clothes gang wanted to see me so bad? Who tipped 'em that I was going to take the Boston express Friday?"

"Not I, sister, not I! Don't forget them gentlemen of the 'office' are wise to your ten thousand-dollar face and figure! I ain't accusing them of brains, but you got no call to hop the joint just when we're wanted bad. Of course they was lookin' for you Friday. And when they pulled you off the sleeper, what happens?"

Gladys Lemoire, known to sundry detective-sergeants of New York by other nomenclature, shrugged a pair of classic shoulders and gazed out over the Hudson from eyes of deepest blue.

"I asked you, what happens?" her brother resumed. "Why, they pinches you — see? Likewise they comes up here and goes through our joint like it was a classy fence. Of course, you was wise that they was goin' to. So was I. That was why you hopped, havin' no brains. Did I do the same? Not Brother Tom. The bulls found me here — monarch of me domains — outraged at the intrusion on me privacy. Yeah, that's me — the innocent householder stall. When they don't find anything here, they can't pull me in. This apartment was a good buy!"

"They didn't find anything?"

"Not a thing. And why? Brother Tom again — soft music with spotlight, please — and his never-failin' head-piece! No, the cops didn't lamp the Hoffman sapphires! They didn't get a chance. The sapphires weren't here."

The woman of the yellow coiffure nodded absently and her eyes narrowed shrewdly. She faced her brother, chin on clasped hands.

"And that's the point. We got to worry about that. The bulls ain't got the Hoffman jewels. All right. But I ain't got them, either."

Lemoire cast a fleeting glance at his sister, and was silent for a calculating moment. Gladys's beautiful face was impassive, but he knew that she seldom showed her thoughts — if it were not advisable.

"Haven't you?" he meditated. "What was the idea of the Boston sleeper, then? I'll go over what happened again — if you've maybe forgot something, sister. First-off, there's you and me at the Charity Ball, real swells, just like in the movie fetes. Close-up of the Hoffman jewels in the necklace worn by old Mrs. S. Van D. Hoffman. You get me, Gladys? This is the way the movies would have it. Sub-title: *fifty thousand bucks' worth of family heirloom.* All right. Another close-up of me and you passing the Hoffman table at supper-time. Business of snipping the gold chain — necklace falls into your cloak. Old-time stuff, that, but good, all the same!"

"I ain't forgotten," amended Gladys.

"Nothing? Well — scene changes. Modern apartment on Riverside, the den of the thieves. Fo Lon, butler of the Lemoires, appears and announces the bulls are all stirred up over the theft — going to raid the apartment on suspicion, just because we was there at the Charity Ball. What's to be done? Close-up of Tom Lemoire outwitting the police. He takes the jewels outa their setting in front of the beautiful vamp — that's you, Gladys — and hides them in the legs of an ivory elephant. Sub-title: *Where will he put the elephant?*"

"It was my idea to send it to Wong Li," observed the woman. "Wong is a good fence; we could trust him. Look here, Torn! Fo Lon couldn't have known the jewels was in the elephant, could he? And we didn't put Wong wise. All we told him, in the message Fo took, was to keep the thing in his shop and not to sell it because we was going to call for it."

"Let me finish me drama," Lemoire settled himself in his chair and lit another cigarette. "Scene showing the bulls giving the apartment the once-over. Nothin' doin'. Lemoire is outraged. Good *Raffles* stuff there, Gladys! The phone rings. Close-up of police-sergeant at Lemoire phone. Sub-title: *Gladys Lemoire is caught in New Haven.*"

The woman leaned back with a smile.

"Did I have the sapphires? The cops didn't find anything on me."

Once more Lemoire's darting glance sought his sister, and his faded eyes closed thoughtfully. Women, he thought, had a way of doing things you could not figure on. Perhaps Gladys did not have the jewels. But the fact that the cops found nothing did not prove it. Lemoire watched her as he talked.

"Scene changes again. Front of Wong's elegant art shop. Crowd rushes into the shop. Sub-title: *Who shot Wong?* Close-up of the shop counter. The elephant is missin'. Loud music and drums. Sub-title: *Ten minutes later.* Flash of beautiful vamp boardin' the train —"

Gladys Lemoire sprang to her feet, her eyes narrowed dangerously.

"Where d'you get that stuff, Tom? You mean to say I did in Wong and got away with that ivory elephant? I can prove I was never in the store that day!"

Lemoire raised a deprecating hand.

"Don't you like my drama, sister? I never said you was in Wong's. I said he was shot — by somebody. We won't get wise to who it is, 'cause we don't get admitted into the hospital, if we dare try. Wong's pretty near kicked in. And Fo ain't here to tell us. Got onto the raid on the apartment, and lays low for a while — maybe in Chinatown.

"Now there's two people *knew* them sapphires was in that elephant. Me and you, sister. The cops had me all the while the shooting was done. Get me? But you was near the spot — got on the train a few minutes later. Likewise — I heard the sergeant talkin' with New Haven over the wire — they found an ivory elephant in your bag. Now, come across, sister. All I want to know is — where are the Hoffman jewels? That's all."

CHAPTER VI.
CROSS-PURPOSES.

The blue in Gladys Lemoire's eyes deepened to the hue of the missing sapphires. Her shapely mouth curved slightly, allowing some of the cigarette-smoke she had in her lungs to issue forth, tracing a hazy spiral to the ceiling. Certain patrons of Broadway taverns would have opened rare, imported wines to see that friendly, faintly malicious smile that Tom Lemoire now saw. Her voice was its gentlest contralto.

"Tom," she responded softly, "you're guessing both ways from the ace. So you're goin' to bawl me, because your fool play lost us the Hoffman sapphires? Ain't you proud of yourself, now, bleating like a sucker? You think I got the sapphires?"

"I know somebody got 'em," retorted Lemoire blandly, "and I know you had the ivory elephant in your bag when the cops found you on the Boston train, sister. All I'm askin' is — put me wise! Let's hear you talk: I'm a good listener."

"Yes — you didn't miss nothing the sergeant said over the wire. Well, I'll tell you just what I did Friday night. I quit the city because I knew the bulls was goin' to watch the Lemoire family for a coupla days, like they loved us. Would I try that if I had those sparklers of yours on me?"

Lemoire made no response beyond a slight shrug. Gladys tucked an errant curl neatly into place, with a glance into the French mirror that took in her brother's sulky face.

"I wasn't fool enough to go near Wong's place. You know he's got a clean slate with the bulls, Tom, and he's treated us well. That Fifth Av'noo joint of his is a swell blind. I went to the train in a taxi and got on the sleeper too late to buy a berth. I sat down in a section with a man I never seen before. After the train started he pulled out his grip and looked at —"

"The ivory elephant, I suppose?"

"That's what he did. I wasn't sure it was ours. But I had to

find out. So when the young gent went to the diner and the porter made up the berth, I pulled the lonesome-lady stuff — said I had to have a berth. I tipped the darky two bucks and he let me stay in the section. The guy's bag was on the berth. I drew the curtains and started to work it open with some of my keys, keeping quiet as I could, naturally.

"The next minute in comes a hand through the curtains with this elephant in it. It gave me the sudden chills, but I saw it wasn't the guy's hand, because it set down this beast and started to feel around the bag for the lock. I tapped it with my keys, and it shot back between the curtains, leavin' the ivory animal — which I grabbed."

Tom Lemoire studied the tracery of smoke hovering about the ceiling, and a sneer crept to his thin lips.

"You learned a lot on the stage, sister. But I got no softenin' of the upper-works —"

"Tom, the elephant that hand dropped wasn't our pachyderm, but it was a whole lot like it."

"Poor stuff, sister. Why didn't you grab the real one in the guy's bag?"

"Because twenty minutes later we was in New Haven and the bulls rushed me off. Besides, the porter came for the bag before I could open it."

"Then what was the dark, mysterious hand doin' with an ivory elephant like the one we had — eh? Them things don't grow twins, that I know of!"

"You know as much about that as I'll tell you."

"Let's see the elephant."

The woman motioned indifferently toward her bedroom, and Lemoire presently returned with her suitcase. From it he took a carved ivory curio.

"Looks like ours," he admitted.

"Sure, I figure somebody else knew the real article was in that bag and tried to get it," assented Gladys, "and plant the dummy, not being wise to the fact I was in the berth."

Lemoire pushed at the animal's eyes and scrutinized its feet with practiced glance. Then he tossed it on the table with an oath. The sneer crept to his eyes.

"I'm damned if I'll let *you* make a sucker out of me, Gladys. You've slipped your cute little tricks over on me too often — just once too often. I got a brain, and that brain tells me what you pulled off on Wong — and me. Listen to Tom, sister! This mysterious gent, who had lower eight, is in with you — one of your gilt-edge boys that you figure to double-cross me with. All right.

"You tip him off about the sapphires and their hidin'-place. He gets the elephant from Wong — shoots him up some — catches the Boston train. I read about the guy with the suitcase in the papers yesterday morning. This cute animal here is a plant — see! Your friend was goin' to switch elephants on Wong, only his play was interfered with. You keep the dummy for future use. And try to string me with this fade-away mystery stuff! Your friend kept the sapphires.

He follows you back to town and hands over the stuff — just to see you smile at him."

Gladys smiled, and Lemoire was not quick enough to read something like triumph in his sister's face.

"If it makes you feel good to think that, I won't quarrel, Tom," she said. "I've done all the explaining I'm goin' to. If you'd trusted Wong more, or not at all, you'd have had the Hoffman stones now. Instead, you half-trusted him. That was your idea. I didn't ask you to try it out. It looked bad to me. Wong wouldn't have put the wheeze on us if he'd known the sapphires was in the elephant. Now they're gone. It's a free-for-all. After your lovin' words, I'll play my hand alone for a while!"

Lemoire halted before her, hands twisting against his sides, eyes narrowed. She paid no attention to him.

"There's fifty thousand bucks' worth of blue stones planted away somewhere, Gladys," he snarled, "and I'll bet the limit you know where!"

"I think I do," she responded.

Her brother's imprecation was cut short by the whir of the telephone. Lemoire jerked up the receiver. His face changed after the first word over the wire.

"It's Fo Lon talkin'," he announced grimly, replacing the receiver. "He's cool-in' his heels in Mott Street — wants to know why the bulls is out after him. I guess they know he's one of our crowd. He wants to see me, Gladys. I'm goin' to chin with him now. I'll get him to see Wong, as soon as it can be done. Today's Sunday. Well, Fo can see Wong by Tuesday, maybe, and I'll know what happened in that shop."

"You'll be wise, then."

Lemoire caught up his hat.

"If Wong tells us," he said slowly, "that this guy who shot him and made the getaway came to his joint lookin' for the ivory elephant there — well, I'll know who tipped him off to it. I ain't forgot, Gladys, that only you and me knew them sapphires was there."

The smile with which the girl watched her brother depart vanished as soon as the door slammed after him. Her face was serious as she sought her suitcase. Taking a slip of paper from her hand-bag, she caught up the telephone directory. She ran through the pages until she came to something that satisfied her. After comparing the slip of paper with the directory she took up the receiver.

CHAPTER VII.
AT MACDOUGAL STREET.

Mrs. Hollis had selected her nephew's rooms for the accommodation of herself and Ruth during their stay in New York for good reasons. The rooms were in Macdougal Street, near the artists' colony of Washington Square — always a spot of interest to visitors—and consisted of a sunny bedroom, sitting-room, and bath. Much to be preferred, thought Mrs. Hollis, to an expensive hotel — especially as she knew her nephew to be well endowed with the neatness of some bachelors of twenty-six. They would find, she told Ruth, every chair and book in the apartment in its place.

So it was with a gasp of surprise that she surveyed the sitting-room when Hollis flung the door open upon their arrival in Washington Square Tuesday noon. Hollis, at her heels, stared and whistled softly. Ruth cast an inquiring glance from the room to him and her aunt.

Neat and orderly the place might have been once. Now, however, the contents of the table lay upon the rug; cigarette ashes strewed the floor. The books in the shelves were piled haphazard where they had once stood in orderly array. A cupboard stood open, disclosing a medley of tobacco tins, pipes, and beer steins.

Mrs. Hollis advanced to the bedroom with compressed lips. The condition of this was even worse. The bedclothes lay in a tousled heap. Garments of masculine gender littered the chairs. She even scented a stale odor of tobacco about the chamber.

"Andy Hollis!" she uttered. "Have you lost every sense of decency? My goodness! To leave your things like this and not tell me about it, when you knew I was bringing Ruth here."

Hollis set down the suitcases he was carrying and glanced about his quarters quizzically. He avoided the eye of Miss Carruthers. Indeed, that young lady had exchanged scarcely a word with him since leaving New Hampshire.

"Remember, Aunt Emma," he responded, "you came here at your own suggestion and risk. However, I assure you I left this place in decent condition. All this must have happened while I was away. Probably some friend has exercised a sense of humor in a rather poor sort of joke."

His aunt dived among the pile of garments on a chair and emerged with a woman's kid glove crumpled into a ball.

"Andy" — her voice echoed genuine surprise — "I never knew a lady to play a joke like this. This glove isn't yours, is it?"

Hollis shook his head, frowning. He felt that Ruth Carruthers was looking at him. Why that should disturb him, he did not know. Somehow he found that his cousin's calm indifference to his presence was disturbing — strangely so, in view of the fact that he cared nothing for her, as he told himself.

"Probably there was a girl with whoever did this," he suggested. "Wild kind of creatures around these diggings on the Square, you know."

Mrs. Hollis sniffed audibly and muttered something about cigarettes. Hollis thought he heard his cousin giggle, but when he glanced at her, Ruth's expression was quite serious. He moved to the telephone and asked the housekeeper to come up.

When Mrs. Henderson presented her bulky, apron-enveloped figure and good-natured Irish face at the door, Hollis pointed to his violated chambers dramatically.

"If this is a house-warming, in honor of my return, Mrs. Henderson," he said grimly, "I'll thank you to assure my aunt of the fact. If not, what kind of a crowd did you let into the apartment?"

Mrs. Henderson's solid jaw dropped and the curtsy she had started for Mrs. Hollis was arrested midway.

"Now, what d'ye think o' that?" she ejaculated. "These rooms was as neat as me own when I showed up your visitor Sunday night."

"My visitor? What was his name?"

The housekeeper shook her head in dumb bewilderment.

"I tell ye, Mrs. Hollis, I never seen the like. We keep this place as clean for Mr. Hollis as yer heart could wish."

"I don't doubt that, Mrs. Henderson," admitted that lady significantly. "It must have been one of his friends, playing a joke."

Mrs. Henderson looked puzzled.

"Now it was a lady I showed up here Sunday night — came in a taxi, and asked if Mr. Hollis was back yet. When I told her no, she said she'd just run up an' leave a note for him, seein' as she was to meet him at the Boston Express Friday an' didn't do it. She said she was afeared he'd be grievin' if she didn't leave the note. Sur-re, I knew Mr. Hollis had took the Boston train, and I thought it was all right."

Hollis ransacked his brain for the identity of a possible feminine correspondent without success. He had always shunned the society of women. Moreover, he had made no appointment with anyone to see him off Friday.

"No one else has been here?"

"Not a soul. I haven't been up mesilf, thinkin' the place was all to rights, an' the key has never left me pocket."

Hollis followed Mrs. Henderson to the door and stepped outside after her, at her summoning nod.

"Whist! Mr. Hollis," she whispered, "I thought I'd best tell ye alone what the lady said — bein' as Mrs. Hollis seems to be distur-rbed. The lady said to tell ye she would like your comp'ny at the Green Pig tearoom on Eighth Street tonight at seven thir-rty. She said it was important."

"Did she give her name?"

"Not a word. She was a big, fine-lookin' blond lady, wearin' furs. I thought ye would know her, now."

"Well, I don't." The description, however, stirred Hollis's memory. Coupled with the mention of the Boston Express, it guided his thoughts to the striking-looking woman who had shared his seat on the sleeper. But she had not known his name. There was the letter he had read, however, within a yard of her. Moreover, he had left the letter addressed to him loosely stuffed in the pocket of his overcoat on the seat.

It was possible that the woman, if she had desired, had learned his name from the letter. But why was she interested in him? Because of the yellow elephant? Again, why?

Suddenly Hollis whistled softly, meditatively The yellow elephant? Worth fourteen dollars and a half, according to Wong Li himself. But *had he put the imitation animal in his bag?* It had been standing beside the valuable Ming curio. In his haste he had scarcely observed the one he had caught up. And they had looked very much alike — to Hollis, who did not know real ivory from the imitation.

Enlightenment flooded on him swiftly.

"The real, good solid ivory is where my brains ought to be," he thought. "Great Scott! The beast I took from Wong Li's was the Ming antique. No wonder Aunt Emma was pleased with it."

Several things were now clear. He recalled the startled shout of Wong Li as he ran from the shop, the assertion of Mrs. Hollis that his gift was a treasure. But there was the attempted theft in the train to be explained. If the light-fingered Oriental had known that he had the Ming antique, the individual in question must have come from Wong Li's shop.

If so, why had he not simply explained the mistake to Hollis and claimed the curio? Then there was the woman of lower eight, who was sufficiently interested to search his apartment. Why? The secret compartments of the curio? Empty. And the shooting of Wong Li?

"As the novels have it, there is more in this than meets the eye," he thought. "And Gladys is the one who can explain it."

Hollis grinned. Here was a woman who appropriated his berth, rifled his baggage, ransacked his apartment, and invited herself to dinner with him. Very well. He would meet her and find out what she wanted. The fact that he was completely in the dark as to what his visitor wanted only clinched his decision. Still, he was not to dine with Ruth. He had vaguely hoped to restore the intimacy between them. It would not be unpleasant to show his pretty cousin the sights of the town. Yes, he knew now that she was pretty.

"I'll have to get in touch with a business transaction," he told his aunt — "and I have an engagement for dinner this evening."

Convinced, as he had suspected, that there was no note left for him in the apartment, he left the two women to restore order in the place, and carried his bag to a nearby French hotel on Fifth Avenue. From there he took the subway to the downtown office of the *News*.

Running through his mail, he came upon a memorandum sheet left on his desk by one of his companions in the office.

He read:

A. HOLLIS (Personal):
    Chinese customer was in Saturday. Wants to buy an ivory curio that you own. Did not leave his name, but will call up Wednesday. Seemed quite anxious to buy.

CHAPTER VIII.
TWO POINTS OF VIEW.

On a side street in one corner of Greenwich Village a painted emblem of a green pig points the way downward to a curtained tearoom in the cellar. The name, Green Pig, is spelled backward, as evidence of eccentricity to attract the wayward tourist. Around the wall, green and pink benches provide seats for a number of small, round tables, minus cloth or paint. A row of impressionistic sketches, for sale to the unwary, surmount the benches. Doll-like manikins hang from the ceiling above the heads of the *literati* of Washington Square. Hollis, who was used to the makeup of the village, took possession of a corner table in the Green Pig at half past seven. A glance showed him that the blond woman of the sleeper was not among the few inmates of the place on his arrival. He ordered a dinner for two, and sat back, lighting his pipe.

His curiosity had grown during the afternoon. So there was a Chinaman in the market for ivory elephants! Apparently, since his visit to Wong Li's, the ivory animals had been in active demand. So much so that after a glimpse of one of the beasts in the Boston train, a blond woman and a brunette Chinaman had gone through his bag to get possession of it.

What puzzled Hollis was the fact that, judging by the expression of the Oriental in the smoking compartment, the man had sighted something of great value. Also — he checked off the point methodically on his fingers — either the Chinaman or the woman, or both, must have followed him in his dash for the train. A second point: the valuable Ming elephant had contained a secret compartment, which proved to be empty.

In spite of all this, the woman in question had undoubtedly searched his apartment — for something. And the Oriental, or another one, was now offering to buy the very elephant that had been placed in his bag. A fifth point: he had forfeited, through no fault of his, the good opinion of Ruth Carruthers. That item was beginning to loom large.

Hollis rose as a tall and well-dressed woman, with blue eyes and a hint of makeup, approached his table. She seated herself with a nod to him and a self-possessed glance around the room.

"Quiet place this," she smiled. "These tourists won't bother us."

Hollis kept silence, waiting for her to speak. When they were half through dinner she leaned forward, chin on hands.

"I figure it's about time we got together, Hollis," she observed. "It may save you some trouble."

"On the contrary, Miss —" He paused suggestively, but she vouchsafed nothing — "as I figure it, you've caused me quite a bit of trouble as it is."

"That's nothin' to what's coming your way," she said calmly. "But maybe I can help you."

"After helping yourself to my bag and my apartment, and causing my landlady to regard me with unwarranted suspicion, I am curious to hear your further offer of assistance, Gladys. I think that's what the police on the Boston train called you."

Gladys produced a cigarette and took one of her companion's matches.

"How d'you get that way, Hollis?" she asked calmly. "After all the trouble I'm taking to do the first-aid act for you? I had to shake one of my crowd to keep this date with you, and you don't like it."

Hollis met her gaze squarely.

"I came here, Gladys, to hear what you had to say to me — if it's worth while. If not, I have other things to do."

"Is it worth while," she asked slowly, "to keep out of prison?"

"To some people, yes. Suppose you show me what you have on your mind."

The girl puzzled Hollis slightly. She was no ordinary adventuress, plying the blackmail game. Yet she seemed sure of her ground. What was her purpose in seeking him? He had little money; certainly he was not good game for her kind.

"All right," she assented. "I'll give you some valuable information. I don't know who you're workin' for, or what you get out of this. But you butted into a layout where you ain't wanted — see? You got hold of something that don't belong to you. I want it. You know what it is without being told. Come across with it, and I got nothin' on you — I'm dumb. How about it?"

"Suppose," suggested Hollis, "you explain a little further."

"Meanin' you want to know what I know? All right. As I said, this something don't belong to you; it's the property of others. And it's worth something. Hand it over. If you don't, what I know gets to the police."

"What do you know, Gladys?"

"Something. I saw you beat it out of Wong Li's Friday when I was goin' to the train in a taxi — the time Wong was shot. And I saw you take out an ivory curio in the car and look at it. That came from Wong's — never mind how — I know that."

"I know as much as that, Gladys," commented Hollis, "without looking into other people's baggage."

"All right. But are you wise that the cops are on to you? You work like a greenhorn. They got hold of some evidence you left behind. My story will fit in well with what they know. Look here, Hollis, my testimony will make things pretty sad for you. I don't want to give it. Hand over what I want, and the cops don't hear a peep from me."

Hollis regarded her quizzically.

"Then, I take it, you think I have something of yours —

that I stole from Wong Li; that the police are looking for the man who shot him, and suspect me. Correct, Gladys?"

"Right. They have the goods on you. I can help you by keeping quiet."

"As it happens, I bought an elephant from Wong. Paid cash for it."

"Got a receipt?"

Hollis was silent. The girl touched his arm.

"How much did you pay for that elephant?" she whispered. "I don't see how you got it away from Wong. He knew it wasn't for sale — and he's quick with his gun."

He grinned cheerfully.

"So it's the elephant you want, Gladys? Well, I paid fourteen dollars and a half for it — told Wong to keep the change. Only the compartments in the legs were empty. I suppose you want whatever was in those concealed cavities? What is it?"

The girl drew in her breath quickly. She carefully studied her companion; then she frowned.

"Do I look that much like a sucker, Hollis? You know what was in the thing. You shot up Wong to get it. There's another guy who's lookin' for the same stuff I am — tried to get it from you in the train. I don't know who he is. I'll give you one more chance. Now you'd better hand over the stuff."

Hollis looked up just as Ruth Carruthers, his aunt, and an elderly, well-dressed man entered the room. They took a table on the farther side of the place, yet a certain stiffness in his aunt's back and Ruth's elaborate indifference showed him that they had seen him.

His first thought was to go over to their table. Then he decided that it would be useless. It was a stroke of ill-luck that brought them to the Green Pig, after he had excused himself from dining with them. The other man, he decided, was the Frenchman whom Ruth had intended to meet.

"Gladys," he said decisively, "I'm not the man who shot Wong Li. And I have nothing of his. The fellow you want is the man who monkeyed with my bag in the sleeper — a

Chinaman. You won't get anything whatsoever from me. Is that clear?"

Out of the corner of his eye, he was aware that the group at the other table were staring at him. He kept his glance grimly fixed on the girl in front of him. Her glance wavered.

"Say — you have nerve. You talk like you wasn't headed for the cooler — but you're the guy they want, all right. And tomorrow they'll know what I know — see? You'll put on the soft pedal when they find fifty thousand bucks' worth of stolen goods on you."

Her tone was bitter, and the warmth had died from her blue eyes, leaving them hard and cold. Hollis glanced at Ruth instinctively, hoping that they had not heard what was said. The sight of the trim, quiet figure of the girl at the other table stirred him. She was smiling at something her companion was saying.

Hollis felt a pang of jealousy. He cursed his unfortunate speech of the other day. Poor relations! The girl was a thoroughbred, and he would have given every dollar he possessed to be sitting in the other man's shoes that minute.

Instead, he paid for the dinners and followed Gladys to the street. Outside the Green Pig he stopped her.

"Look here, Gladys," he said, "you may be right, and I may be in the devil's own mess over this ivory elephant. But I have one card up my sleeve you don't know about."

"What's that?" the woman asked, with quick curiosity.

"A clear conscience," he grinned. "Good night, Gladys."

CHAPTER IX.
NEGOTIATIONS.

The next morning went badly for Hollis. At the office he found his thoughts straying from trade and market statistics to a dark-eyed, dark-haired girl who treated him with queenly indifference. The sight of Ruth in the Green Pig had made it clear to him that she would never be absent from his thoughts — that he was held fast by the charm of a low, Southern voice and a wonderful pair of frank, friendly brown eyes.

The telephone at his elbow whirred, and he picked up the receiver.

"This is Mr. Hollis?" a man's hesitating voice asked, with a curious lisp.

"I am Hollis: who is this?"

There was a brief pause. Then —

"I want to buy an ivory curio that you own, Mr. Hollis. I am a collector. It is an old ivory Ming elephant with very delicious carving. I am greatly in desire of it. You will sell?"

Hollis had forgotten the Chinese customer who had promised to call him up. This was he, judging by the twisted, Oriental English of the speaker.

"I might be willing to sell the Ming elephant," Hollis assured him, reflecting that his purchase was in growing demand, and wishing to draw out the Oriental further. "What price will you give me? Your best figure."

Another silence followed.

"Five hundred dollars for the elephant and stand," vouchsafed the voice at length.

"Not enough."

"Six hundred."

"I have taken up collecting lately, Mr. —," grinned the newspaperman. "I also am enamored of the delicious carving. The Ming elephant is a wonderful specimen. I don't know that I want to sell at all."

"Eight hundred dollars. I need it, Mr. Hollis, to complete my series of Ming ivories."

"So do I."

"One thousand dollars for the elephant and stand."

"Wait a minute."

Hollis leaned the receiver against his ear and reflected. Obviously the man at the other end of the wire was aware of the secret value of the antique. Gladys had mentioned fifty thousand dollars. Where the great value of the elephant lay Hollis did not know. Certainly he and Ruth had made a thorough search of the curio.

But the man at the other end of the wire knew the explanation of the mystery. He could tell Hollis — or be made to tell The fact that the ivory elephant reposed on his aunt's what-not in the parlor at New Hampshire would not prevent him from getting in touch with the Oriental.

"I might be willing to sell at that figure," Hollis said slowly. "Suppose you meet me somewhere and we'll talk it over — tonight."

The other pondered over the proposition for a moment.

"All right, Mr. Hollis. Be at Chinese Delmonico's, Pell Street, in the upper room. Ten o'clock. You will come?"

"I'll come."

He hung up as the other started to say something about bringing the elephant with him. Chinatown, reflected Hollis, was an unusual place for curio collectors — which agreed with his suspicion that the other was no collector, but one of the crowd looking for the missing valuables.

Hollis dismissed the matter from his mind, picked up his hat, and took the subway uptown. He sought Washington Square and the door of his apartment house. He would see Ruth, he thought, and make a clean breast of things.

At the door of the building, however, he found Mrs. Henderson, who approached him with a worried look.

"Miss Carruthers says she ain't to home, Mr. Hollis."

He stared at the housekeeper blankly.

"Is Miss Carruthers in?"

"Yes, sir. They have a gentleman caller — a fine-lookin' man in one of them flyaway suits. But the young lady and her aunt said to tell you they wasn't in, if you called."

"Confound it, Mrs. Henderson — do you mean I can't go

up to my own rooms?"

The housekeeper's good-natured face clouded sympathetically. Evidently Hollis's aunt had spoken very plainly.

"They said if you wanted anything of yours they'd be glad to send it down by me, sir."

The humor of the situation struck Hollis, and he grinned. Going to the switchboard by the door, he asked to be connected with his apartment. Ruth answered his call.

"Good morning, cousin," said Hollis amiably. "Hope you had a pleasant night"

"Thank you, Mr. Hollis," her soft voice responded coolly. "We did have a right nice sleep. I trust we did not interfere with your — business transaction last night. Professor de Bacourt, to whom I had that letter of introduction, was kind enough to take us out to dinner. The professor is a charming gentleman. Aunt Emma is quite in love with him."

Hollis mentally consigned the professor to other regions.

"It was about last night," responded Hollis doggedly, "that I wanted to see you, Cousin Ruth. I owe you an apology for leaving you. But I had to see that person. In fact, I'm involved in quite a serious mess. I may be locked up on a charge of robbery in the next few hours."

He waited breathlessly for the girl's response.

"Why, that is too bad, Mr. Hollis," she said coldly. "Aunt Emma had promised that you would show us all over New York, I've been wanting to see it for years. Professor de Bacourt has been too kind. He is going to take us to Chinatown tonight. To the — Chinese Delmonico's. That's the name, isn't it? Aunt Emma has a cold, but I reckon I can go without a chaperon just this once."

He wondered if he had heard aright. Surely the girl could not be so indifferent to his own plight! And to go to Chinatown alone —

"Do you think that's safe, Ruth?" he asked anxiously. "You don't know anything about this professor chap. He may be all right — but I don't want you to run any risk, in this city —"

"Why, Mr. Hollis," she broke in indignantly, "Professor de Bacourt is a distinguished Orientologist, known to the best people in New Orleans. He is a talented Frenchman and a very charming gentleman."

Hollis gritted his teeth and cursed the breed of ivory elephants from alpha to omega.

"What did you say, Mr. Hollis?" asked Ruth demurely. "It sounded right like a cuss word to me. I don't think you should use such language. Professor de Bacourt wouldn't."

The newspaperman took a long breath.

"Look here, cousin," he demanded. "I'm in trouble, unexpected trouble. Things may break badly for me. I don't want to spoil your enjoyment of the sights of the town. But I'd like to see you to explain things. I never meant that idiotic remark at Aunt Emma's to apply to you — and there are a lot of things I want to talk over. I think," he smiled grimly, "that a lady should give a gentleman a chance to apologize if he asks for it nicely. That's what they usually do in New Orleans, isn't it?"

"Well —" the girl's soft voice hesitated. Hollis thought he caught a smothered laugh.

"And I seem to be mixed in a gang of robbers here," he added, hoping to enlist her sympathy.

"Did you see yesterday's paper, Mr. Hollis?" Ruth's voice was cold again.

"Good Lord, no!" he groaned. "What's happened now?"

"Mrs. Hoffman," explained the girl precisely, "offers a thousand dollars' reward and no questions asked for the return of her sapphire stones. The story in the paper a week ago said that they were worth fifty thousand. You see, it's a habit of us poor country folks to read your New York papers. And don't you think it might be well to return the sapphires before it's too late?"

Hollis blinked. He had noted the newspaper account of the robbery. And the figure named was fifty thousand dollars — by Gladys and now by Ruth. It was barely possible that the Hoffman sapphires might be the valuables wanted by the Oriental gang and blond Gladys. But how were the jewels connected with ivory elephants; and what in the name of absurdities did his cousin know about it all?

"I thought," she went on quietly, "that the information might be of service to your — friends. You see, Mr. Hollis, I don't know anything about how you-all do things in New York."

"Of course not! That is — you don't really think I've got the Hoffman sapphires, do you, Ruth?" His voice took on an appealing note.

"Why, I don't *guess* so, Cousin Hollis," she drawled. "But you said that you were so involved in a robbery — I —"

"Great Scott, Ruth! I'm beginning to believe I have them, after all. That is — that Aunt Emma has. No, that couldn't be. Look here," he groaned, "I can't explain all this over the phone. Why can't you let me see you, Ruth? Shake the professor tonight. I'll make a counter proposition. We'll go to dinner at Guffarone's and to the best show in town afterward."

"Professor de Bacourt could chaperon us."

"No — I must see you alone, Ruth. Supper after the show, anywhere you like. Dancing — I know you are a great little dancer."

He waited anxiously for her response.

"It does sound attractive," she meditated. "I love dancing. And I've heard so much about the New York cafés —"

"I'll come in a taxi for you at seven!" Hollis closed the bargain swiftly. "I'll send up word — if Aunt Emma doesn't want to see me — for you."

He left the switchboard, directed Mrs. Henderson to have his evening clothes, hat, and stick sent to the near-by hotel, and returned to the office exultantly. From there he reserved a table at Guffarone's and two seats for a fashionable musical comedy. Not until then did he stop to wonder if his conversation over the telephone had not convinced Ruth Carruthers that he was a professional gangster, with a penchant for jewelry.

CHAPTER X.
CLOSING THE NETS.

At six thirty that evening Tom Lemoire entered the elaborate facade of the Riverside Drive apartment without waiting for the elevator he ascended the stars three at a time to the Lemoire rooms. In the parlor he found Gladys dozing. At her brother's hasty entrance she roused with an inquiring glance.

"Move swiftly, sister," snapped Lemoire. "Get your bag packed. The Lemoire family is leaving town tonight. I got a buzz over the wire from one of Wong's men. The bulls have traced the Hoffman stones, somehow. Traced 'em to us."

As Gladys hurried into her room and began throwing articles into a suitcase, she talked.

"We ain't got 'em."

"No — but the bulls are wised that we had 'em at the Charity Ball."

Gladys's mouth curled in a sneer.

"I thought you and Fo Lon was going to get the stones, Tom."

Lemoire swore under his breath.

"Fo Lon is through with us — quit, see? He's hangin' out in Chinatown. Wouldn't go to see Wong. He said we left him out in the cold over them sapphires. Fo Lon told me something. He was in Wong's when the shooting was pulled off. Followed a guy who grabbed the Ming elephant, to the Boston train. Wanted to get even for the shooting, I expect; all them Chinks is nuts on squaring accounts —"

"Then it was Fo Lon tried to switch elephants through the curtains of lower eight," guessed Gladys swiftly. "How'd he get the dummy?"

"What the — does that matter? He ain't got the sparklers — or he wouldn't be tryin' to get hold of the guy he followed out of Wong's. I ain't got 'em. I'm beginnin' to think you ain't got em —"

"Thanks," smiled the girl coldly. "Listen, Tom. A fellow named Hollis was in Wong's the time of the shooting. He's got the other elephant, and the stones. I tipped off the cops about him. They'll get after him before they tackle us. We got time —"

"About two minutes. I tell you, the cops or Mrs. Hoffman have traced the stones. They're on to us — somehow. We're leaving New York — first stop Buffalo, then Toronto, if we ain't pinched, and our luck holds —"

Gladys ran to the window and looked out. A touring car bearing three men in plain clothes was swinging in to the curb by the building. She waited long enough to see that all three went into the front entrance. Then she called to Tom, snapped out the lights of the rooms, and made for the servant's entrance of the apartment.

A rear stairway for servants led down to the court behind the building. The Lemoires descended this in safety. The court opened into a side street. There they sighted a taxi.

At seven o'clock the Lemoires were installed on a fast, north-bound train.

And at seven o'clock, precisely, Andrew Hollis, immaculately dressed, halted his taxi before the apartment house in Washington Square. He waited impatiently in the street for Ruth's coming.

Here was his opportunity to clear up the muddle of circumstances that had estranged him and Ruth. He thought, with a quickening of the pulse, that she had broken her engagement with the professor to be with him. It would be an evening to be remembered, showing the night life of the city to his cousin from New Orleans. He might even have a chance to tell her —

He greeted her with a strange shyness. Ruth had evidently been visiting one of the shops. She wore a dark-red cloak, tipped with fur, that harmonized with her dark hair. Her eyes were bright with all a girl's expectancy of an evening's entertainment. As he helped her into the taxi a hand fell on his shoulder.

"You're wanted at police headquarters, Hollis."

He whirled and saw two men with bulky shoulders and clean-shaven faces standing beside him.

"Wanted?" he demanded. "For what? Have you a warrant?"

"We got a warrant," announced the speaker. "Sorry to take you away from the lady. But there's some things you got to explain."

The girl leaned forward and watched the three anxiously. Hollis felt the touch of her gloved hand on his arm. He shrugged his shoulders, remembering what Gladys had said.

"As a favor to me," he asked calmly, "would you tell me what I'm wanted for and why? I've never been arrested before and I'd like to understand the procedure from the first."

The plain-clothes men glanced at each other.

"Well — if you want to know," said the first speaker, "we got you on two counts. First, you was in Wong Li's shop at the time he was shot — and left an envelope that looked like a pay envelope with your name on it. You left in a hurry and quit the burg. Then you come back to another hotel — not to your rooms. Since Gladys Lemoire tipped us off, we been watching you, Hollis."

"And the second count?" he inquired, with a sinking heart.

"Well, Gladys spilled the dope you knew something

about the stolen Hoffman sapphires. Said you had 'em. If you haven't, you can clear it up easy. Just come along with us."

"Just a minute," assented Hollis. He met the girl's anxious glance squarely, and cut off her quick protest. He gave her the envelope containing the theater tickets.

"I'll have to keep this date with the police, Ruth," he grinned. "But that needn't spoil your evening. Call up De Bacourt and get him to take you to the show. Don't worry about me."

He waved his hand and moved off between the detectives. If he had looked back he would have seen that the girl was watching him with flushed face and eyes in which gleamed a suspicion of tears. It occurred to Hollis presently to make a suggestion to his escort. Wong Li, he explained, could tell them, if he was faced with Hollis, that the latter was not the man who shot him.

"Yeah," assented his conductor indifferently. "He could if you could see him. Wong Li left the hospital alone an' unexpectedly, sick as he was. We ain't able to locate him. Those Chinks are scared of the law."

"Well, there's Gladys Lemoire — if that's her name," suggested Hollis. "Get her, and I'll convince you she's lying."

"She an' Tom 've flown the coop — beat it outa the burg. Maybe we can land 'em in a week, maybe not. P'r'aps you'll tip us where they are. We know you're in thick with 'em. They lifted the stones an' passed 'em on to you."

Hollis breathed a malediction on the vagaries of fate that had led him to Wong Li's and the Ming antique.

"Look here!" he cried, "I can prove I wasn't at the Charity Ball, where those jewels were stolen. And Mrs. Hoffman can tell you she's never seen me. All you have against me is the word of a woman crook."

"No, not all, Hollis," the man shook his head. "The stones was returned to Mrs. Hoffman yesterday by a friend who didn't claim the reward. He said he got 'em away from you. His name is Professor de Baycoor. Look here, sport, Mrs. Hoffman is raising hell about that stone lifting. We got to have something to show her for what we been doin' — see. We want the Lemoires — they musta done the trick at the Char'ty Bazoo. But, likewise, we wants you, too."

CHAPTER XL
DE BACOURT EXPLAINS.

At court, Hollis learned a number of things. First, as Wong Li was not there to appear against him — had, in fact, said nothing as to the identity of the man who shot him — the count of the shooting failed to hold him. On the other hand he was faced with a network of circumstantial evidence regarding the theft of the Hoffman sapphires — evidence which pointed to the fact that he had been an accomplice of the Lemoires. Evidence not less portentous because of his knowledge of how he had taken the Ming elephant from Wong.

He learned that Mrs. Hoffman's telephone message to the police had stated that Professor de Bacourt had restored the jewels to her, alleging that they had been found in his — Hollis's — personal baggage. Nothing more than that was known.

"If It had not been for the information from Gladys Lemoire," he was told, "there would be no warrant out for you, because Mrs. Hoffman did not accuse you of the theft of the jewels. You have established a valid alibi, proving that you were not present at the Charity Ball, where the sapphires were stolen. Probably through Mrs. Hoffman, or Mr. de Bacourt, you can clear yourself of all suspicion."

Hollis reflected grimly that Gladys had made good her threat — and that she was at present beyond reach. He began to be convinced that he had had the missing jewels in his possession. But where? And how had they been removed from him?

With the wisdom of a newspaperman in dealing with the law, Hollis denied everything, and then kept his mouth shut. It cost him three hours, the presence of his friends on the *News*, and three thousand-dollar bonds before he was admitted to bail and allowed to leave the court, pending arraignment.

Hollis jumped into a taxi, directed the man to Chinatown, and glanced at his watch. It was quarter to eleven.

Ruth had said, he reflected, that De Bacourt would take her to Chinatown late that evening. Probably they would go there from the theater, about now. He wanted to see De Bacourt, and learn the part the latter had played in the affair of the jewels. Vague suspicion flooded upon him.

De Bacourt had been assiduous in his attentions to Ruth. Had he planned to keep Hollis from his cousin? Why had he gone to Chinatown that night? A slow anger rose in Hollis, and fastened upon him. He would find out what De Bacourt knew. And then he would order the man out of Ruth's presence. The girl was unacquainted with the city and

the ways of its men. She might be in danger that minute. And he, Hollis, was her champion.

He left the machine at the door of the Chinese Delmonico's and sought through the restaurant purposefully. The two he wanted were not there, but he remembered the room upstairs, and ascended to its lacquered and latticed privacy.

In a corner, screened from the rest of the room, he found Ruth Carruthers, a middle-aged man in evening dress, and a Chinaman. He wondered fleetingly if this was the man who had come to buy the ivory elephant. The Oriental, however, was heavily bandaged about the head, and pale. His cousin sprang to her feet with a cry.

She wore an evening dress of dark brown which accentuated the white of arms and throat. Hollis saw that her eyes lighted warmly as she caught his hand. He glared hostilely at the other, who had risen courteously. He saw a striking-looking individual, evidently a foreigner, with monocle and carefully tended mustache.

"Oh, I'm so glad!" cried the girl. "They have let you go, haven't they, Andy?"

Hollis scowled.

"No thanks to this gentleman that they have," he said shortly. "May I ask what he is doing here alone with you at this time of night, Ruth? Now that your aunt is sick, I consider myself your guardian."

Ruth laughed suddenly, deliriously; the Frenchman smiled. Hollis scowled the more.

"Why, Andy!" she exclaimed, "you know you told me to invite M. de Bacourt to the theater." Her voice softened quickly. "It was — was right splendid of you, when you were in such trouble. I would have gone with you, only M. de Bacourt said they would release you at once. And we had to come here so that *monsieur* could see Wong Li. Wong has been here, waiting for someone ever since he left the hospital."

Hollis's glance flew to the Oriental. The bandage had kept him from recognizing Wong Li. He seated himself beside the girl at the table and stared blankly at the other three.

"You had no trouble, I hope," observed the professor in fair English, "in satisfying the police? I made it clear to Mrs. Hoffman that you had assisted me in recovering her sapphires."

"She failed to make that clear to the police," retorted Hollis. "And the Lemoire gang gave some information against me."

"Ah, that I did not know. A word from me will release you," said the Frenchman quickly. "I regret that we could not have appeared before the police, but we had important information to get from Wong Li."

"More important than keeping me out of a cell?"

Hollis glanced from the impassive face of the Chinaman to the others.

"Suppose," he suggested to De Bacourt, "that you tell me three things. You seem to know what's happening to me. First — why I am accused of shooting Wong Li, when I am fully aware that I never did anything of the kind. Second — why I am credited with the possession of valuable jewelry that I have never laid eyes on. Third — why you and my cousin know more about my affairs than I do."

"They think you shoot me?" Wong Li spoke suddenly. "That must be because you visit at my shop two minutes before somebody else shoot at me. You left an envelope there — eh? They find that, other man fire at me and run out with suitcase, just same you."

"All right," nodded Hollis. He caught Ruth's glance on him and was surprised to read warm sympathy in her expressive face.

"Andy," she said impulsively, "you must forgive me for treating you the way I did. But you were so — so mean to me at Aunt Emma's when I tried to win your confidence —"

De Bacourt leaned forward smilingly.

"It is a riddle for you, is it not, *monsieur*? You do not know me? I am a professor of the college where *mademoiselle* hopes to study. Also, I have some knowledge of the Orient, and — what you call — a fad for the psychology of the East — the criminal mind. Wong Li is known to me — he has often sold me antiques. *Eh bien,* on Monday *mademoiselle* appeared before me with a tale of distress, and a note to introduce. In a gift from you to your aunt she had found a collection of valuable sapphires."

Hollis turned to his cousin in surprise. She nodded.

"You remember the ivory elephant, Andy. When you said someone had tried to steal it, I was curious. I love Oriental puzzles, and before long I found the concealed pockets which contained a dozen splendid sapphires. I couldn't imagine how they got there. I took them out to test you — see if you would miss them. I saw about Wong Li's injury in the paper, and I knew that you had bought it at his store.

"It was such an exciting mystery, and you were so rude, I couldn't ask your help. When you said you paid only fifteen dollars for it, and snubbed me, I guessed you knew nothing about the jewels. But I was real mad at you. So I went to *monsieur* for advice."

Into Hollis's memory flashed the repeated demand of his unknown customer.

"I was just all on fire with curiosity," continued Ruth eagerly, "because I reckoned the sapphires were those stolen from Mrs. Hoffman. When I took them to Professor de Bacourt, Monday, he offered to restore them to Mrs. Hoffman, whom he knew. Then he promised to take me to Wong Li and find out how the jewels came to be in the elephant."

"*Monsieur,*" interrupted De Bacourt, with a humorous lift of the eyebrow, "the curiosity of a woman and a running brook are alike. Both have no end."

Wong Li's heavy voice broke in on him.

CHAPTER XII.
THE LAST WORD.

"I tell you how that happen," he said. "You listen. Monday afternoon Fo Lon, butler fellow for Miss Lemoire, who are good customer with me, come to my shop. He bring ivory elephant with stand, much like one I had, and tell me to keep it for Miss Lemoire, not to sell. So I put too high price on Miss Lemoire's Ming elephant."

"I know you did," nodded Hollis, who was beginning to see light.

"Yes, Mr. Hollis. This fellow Fo Lon him suspect valuables hidden in Ming elephant — hear Miss Lemoire talking to brother. So we look. Chinaman has good eyes." He smiled fleetingly. "We find jewels, Fo Lon and I. Fo Lon said Lemoires stole sapphires. Just then you come in door and we put elephant with jewels back on stand, to be secretly hidden. I watch, because Fo Lon is low-caste thief, without honor. Then you buy other, inferior animal."

"When Wong went back for your change," interrupted the girl eagerly, "neither Wong nor Fo suspected at first you had the one with the jewels, you took one of the elephants and ran out. Fo Lon seized the chance to carry off what he thought was the Ming curio — which he put in his suitcase. Wong tried to prevent him, and Fo Lon shot him, wounding him in the head. Then Fo Lon must have run to the railway station around the corner, and taken the first train out, which was the same you were on."

"And incidentally tried to break into my suitcase when he found out that he had the wrong beast — knowing I must have the other," concluded Hollis. "By the way, that's what started Gladys Lemoire on my trail. She saw me looking at my purchase in the car, and recognized it."

Wong Li raised his hand blandly.

"Fo Lon," he said somberly, "is one who betrayed both his master and his friend — myself. Evil comes to those without honor."

Hollis laughed.

"All clear," he assented. "I had the jewels in *my* bag all the time — Great Scott! That's why when Fo Lon found out the mistake he made he tried to get me to sell him my elephant and stand when he returned to town. I'll bet Fo Lon's the one who was going to meet me here to bargain for it."

He smiled at the girl, whose eyes were dancing with excitement. The room echoed with the murmur of voices, and the pad-pad of silk-clad waiters, De Bacourt's smile faded as Wong Li turned to Hollis, dark eyes narrowed to a pinpoint, his slender hands clenched on the table.

"Fo Lon will be here to meet you?" Wong asked softly. "Tonight?"

"He's late now," nodded Hollis carelessly. Then he glanced at Wong Li's intent face again. The Chinaman had a blood score to settle with Fo Lon. The man looked like a snake about to strike, he thought. And a Chinaman goes about revenging an injury with almost a religious fervor of fanaticism. He glanced toward De Bacourt, who had also noted the Oriental's change of expression. Hastily the Frenchman called a waiter.

"I wonder why, Andy," said the girl mischievously, heedless of the by-play, "I thought all along you were innocent. But you did make it hard for me — when you went to meet that blond Lemoire girl. I reckon it was because I hated her so."

Hollis's reply was frozen on his lips. He heard De Bacourt's muttered exclamation — saw Wong Li's right hand steal toward his capacious left sleeve. The Frenchman rose, but Hollis had heard Wong's sibilant indrawing of breath, and was before him. Sliding around the table, he caught up the girl bodily in her chair and swung her away from the table. As he did so two shots echoed through the room.

Hollis's glance flew from Wong, crouched over the table, a blue revolver smoking in his hand, to another Chinaman reeling to the floor, weapon in hand, a few yards away.

It was the Chinaman who had been his companion in the smoking compartment. Wong Li's score was settled.

"Take her to the street; I'll follow," cried De Bacourt in his ear.

Through the alarmed crowd that stumbled from the upper floor of the Chinese Delmonico's to the street, Hollis carried the startled girl. Finding a taxi at Mott and Pell Street, he put her inside and waited for De Bacourt.

He was forced to admire the calmness of the Frenchman. De Bacourt appeared, quietly bearing Hollis's hat and coat, and bowed to Ruth.

"*Monsieur,*" he said gravely, "I owe *mademoiselle* a thousand pardons for that unfortunate scene. The fact that I did not suspect Fo Lon would be there does not excuse my fault. My only consolation is that she is now in better hands than mine."

With that he kissed Ruth's gloved hand ceremoniously, bowed politely to Hollis, and departed down the crowded street, swinging his stick jauntily.

Hollis turned to the silent girl at his side and drew a deep breath.

"Professor de Bacourt is all right, Ruth," he said; "but he's mistaken if he thinks he will have you for a pupil."

She laughed a trifle unsteadily.

"Why, Andy, that's what I came here for."

But he had seen the startled look, aftermath of the scene in the restaurant, replaced by a shy light in her eyes.

"No, you didn't," he corrected happily. "You came here to see the sights of New York — after you've married me."

SEA SONG
by Nelson S. Bond

I stood on a quay by the edge of the sea
And watched the ships come in.
There were long ships, and strong ships,
And wallowing ships, and thin.
I wondered about the men who sailed, and the kinds of lives they led,
And I met a sailor from Halifax, and this is what he said,

>*"Keep away from the sea, my lad,*
>*Keep away from the sea.*
>*Take a wife, and lead a life*
>*As cozy as it can be.*
>*Swing a hoe and plant a row*
>*But take a tip from me;*
>*Keep away from the sea, my lad,*
>*Keep away from the sea."*

But the gulls wheeled, and the ropes screeled,
And the tar scent reeked in the air;
And I looked at the holds and hatches
And I thought of the treasures there.
I wondered what would happen if a man should put to sea,
And I met a sailor from Liverpool, and this he said to me,

>*"Keep away from the sea, my lad,*
>*Keep away from the sea.*
>*Wield a mop, or buy a shop,*
>*Or carry a watchman's key.*
>*Work in a bank, of fill a tank,*
>*But take this tip from me;*
>*Keep away from the sea, my lad,*
>*Keep away from the sea."*

But the sails had begun to shake in the sun,
And whiter than white were they.
They whipered a tune from old Rangoon
With words from far Cathay.
I thought of the lives of shorebound men, and I wondered what I'd miss,
And I met a sailor from Sicily, and he frowned as he told me this;

>*"Keep away from the sea, my lad,*
>*Keep away from the sea.*
>*Slave in a mill, or guard a till,*
>*Or bank in guarantee . . .*
>*Work for the rich, or dig a ditch,*
>*But take this tip from me;*
>*Keep away from the sea, my lad,*
>*Keep away from the sea."*

And I listened and heard 'most every word
That the sailors told to me,

Yet I suddenly knew that each man in the crew
Was as happy as he could be.
So I packed up my bag, and I said goodbye, and that night I sailed away,
And now, whenever I meet a youth, I too can grin and say,

"Keep away from the sea, my lad,
Keep away from the sea.
Play in a band, or plow the land,
Or sell imported tea.
Work in a Bourse, or drive a horse,
But take this tip from me;
Keep away from the sea, my lad,
Keep away from the sea!"

Oh, Clouded Crystal Ball! — An introduction to "Shall Stay These Couriers . . ."
by Nelson S. Bond

One of the questions most frequently asked a writer is "Where do you get the ideas for your storues?" In my current Arkham House book, Other Worlds Than Ours, I have once replied to this query, but I now think of yet another answer. "From my hobbies!"

The pursuit of a hobby so enthralls an individual that he not only becomes a slave to its demands; at the same time he so deeply studies it that he becomes its master. Or so, at least, it was for me. Hobbies became not only a part of my daily life, they became a part of my livelihood. A devotee of chess , I wrote several chess stories. A bowler, I wrote tales about that pastime. And an avid collector of Canadian stamps, I researched and published two definitive books on obscure aspects of Canadian philately: The Federal Revenue Stamps of Canada and The Postal Stationery of Canada. Both of these for pure love of the hobby. But I also wrote and in 1940 sold to Thrilling Wonder Stories the space epic here reprinted for the first time, a tale about a philatelic rarity issued on a distant satellite one hundred and seventy years in the future!

Oh, clouded crystal ball! How could I have been so short-sighted? Or so erroneously long-sighted? The stamp about which I wrote had a face value of only ten cents, and the postal courier covering his appointed rounds was piloting an interplanetary spacecraft in the year 2112!

So whatever the story's entertainment value, I goofed! And for this optimistic fault forgive me. But when doing so remember, I am by no means the first author who got himself hopelessly tangled in a time trap. The talented Ignatius Donnelly, who gave us such marvelous books as Atlantis: the Antedeluvian World and Ragnarok: the Age of Fire and Gravel, also in the 1880s published a book titled *Caesar's Column* in which he portrayed a New York City of the future in which there would be tall buildings in which were little rooms that ran up and down to carry passengers to the various floors; a New York from which would daily depart in aircraft passengers to the cities of Europe. A populous metropolis in which there would only be one major problem: that there would scarcely be enough space to stable all the horses!

But enough of this preliminary chatter! Now get on with the story!

NELSON S. BOND.

"SHALL STAY THESE COURIERS . . ."
by Nelson S. Bond

Zach Wheatley turned away from the perilens, his mouth creasing into a pucker. A slow, brown stream arced languidly across the control turret of the *Spica*, rocking the cuspidor.

"Iris, three points off the starboard vane," he said. "As if you didn't know."

Russ Hodges, S. S. P. lieutenant now on special duty as pilot-commander of the *Spica*, stifled a Discipline, he realized, was all on a war rocket or patrol ship. He had long since given up trying to convert Wheatley. He touched the controls on the panel before him.

"Braces locked," Wheatley called. "Fore jets fire!"

"Fore jets it is!"

"Extend luggers!"

Wheatley shoved his sturdy against a lever.

"Extend luggers it is!"

"Very good. Stand by." Russ rammed in the switch activating the pilot's perilens. On the visiplate sprang the image of a tiny, crudely spherical chunk of rock that was the asteroid Iris. Scarcely a hundred and fifty miles in diameter, Iris was a drab and desolate place, a mining outpost of the Inter-galactic Metals Corporation.

As Russ watched, fingers poised over the controls, the asteroid foreshortened, became a flattened saucer of stone. The ship shuddered violently from stem to stern as the lugsail wings slid from their retracting ports and gripped the tenuous atmosphere of the planetoid. Wheatley, staring through the master lens, grunted his approval.

"Landing field below," he announced.

Russ saw the glistening metal hut on the edge of an arid plain. He saw the sudden flare of smoke that served as his "all clear" landing signal. When he saw the tiny, bulger-clad figure that ran from the hut to wave a delighted greeting, he cut all jets and threw the *Spica* into a closing spiral.

"Got their bag ready?" he asked Zach.

"Yep."

"Yes, sir!" reminded Russ. "Watch the formalities, Zach. While we're down there, I mean. I don't give a blast in space while we're alone, but—"

"Yes, *sir*!" grinned his assistant.

"And Zach," Russ gestured toward the huge cud in Wheatley's cheek. "Unload the cargo. The tobacco, I mean."

"Nicotians to you," said Zach.

He sauntered to the gabboon and unloaded his chew agreeably. Then he broke two bulgers from the locker, tossed one to his superior, and climbed into the other himself.

"Might as well put it on," he advised. "Plaice is a dope.

Like as not, he'll come in and smell up the place with ammonia fumes."

Russ nodded and donned his own space-suit. Just as he finished, there came a grinding jar. The *Spica* bounced, jolting both men back on their heels, then settled. Almost immediately the air-lock warning buzzed and they heard the asthmatic wheeze which meant someone was entering the ship.

"Right again, Zach," said Russ. He closed his face port. Wheatley did the same. A few seconds later, the door of the control turret swung open. Plaice, Superintendent of the IGMC and official postmaster of the Iris station, bustled in, his face wreathed in a huge smile.

"Greetings, Captain!" he bubbled. "Welcome to Iris again. Any mail for us this trip? We're hoping—" He stopped suddenly, staring at Hodges. "Why, you're not Captain French!"

"He's psychic!" growled Zach Wheatley.

Russ silenced him with a glance.

"No," he said. "I'm Lieutenant Russell Hodges, Solar Space Patrol. On special detail, Mr. Plaice."

Plaice showed his disappointment. "We thought it was the mail ship —" he began.

"It is," nodded Russ. "We're carrying mail. I'll explain it all to you in your office. Wheatley, bring along the Iris mail, will you?"

"Aye—*sir!*" The last was an afterthought.

Wheatley tossed a slim pouch over his shoulder and followed the two men as they left the *Spica*. They walked across a few rods of Iris soil, and ducked into the doorway of the mine superintendent's office.

"There are two reasons," Lt. Russ Hodges explained, "why I'm covering Captain French's mail route for him this trip. One of them is rather amusing. It would be, except that it's causing a mild panic in the Postal Service. The other is more serious. It is—piracy!"

"Piracy?" Plaice repeated blankly.

"You've heard of Balder Sorenson, haven't you? The pirate who was exiled to the penal colony on Uranus a couple of years ago? Well, he has escaped. Don't ask me how. We don't know. The fact remains that he has escaped. He has gathered together some of his old crew, and is now terrorizing space-lanes between Jupiter and Venus. But he doesn't have a large ship, like in the old days. He's using a small speedster. Consequently he's preying on the kind of craft that carry valuables in small bulk."

"Only," interjected Wheatley sourly, "he stuck his neck

out too far. He held up the *Spica* on its last trip and there ain't nobody can do the P. O. that-away."

Plaice looked at the SSP officer questioningly, and Russ nodded.

"Precisely. That was a vital error on Sorenson's part. The police may be a little slow sometimes when it comes to apprehending criminals. But when bandits attack the mail—" He grinned, "Well, you know the traditions of the Post Office Department. Almost three hundred years old, but the mail must still go through."

"Yes, I know," Plaice said. "Something else about 'swift couriers'?"

"'Nor rain,'" quoted Russ softly, "'nor snow, nor heat, nor gloom of night, stays these couriers from the swift completion of their appointed rounds.' That's the motto of the Post Office Department. They held it way back in the days when foot-runners and the pony express carried the mail, then when the first airships hobbled along like winged snails.

"It still holds good today. Men on Venus, Mars, on the farthest outposts of Uranus and Pluto — men like yourself, lonely on spinning rocks no bigger than a mountain on Earth, depend on the postal service. For news from loved ones at home. For contact with a world they may not have seen for years. For money, payment for their labors —"

He grimaced. "The last is why Sorenson waylaid the *Spica*. A lot of valuables are entrusted to the mails. Actual cash. Negotiable stocks. Bullion of rare metals. It's estimated that Sorenson's haul netted him a cool quarter million."

"A quarter million!" Plaice whistled. "Do you mean Venus dollars?"

"Earth! You see, now, why I've been assigned to this trip. Maybe you can't notice, but the *Spica* has been converted into a miniature man-o'-war. Rotor guns fore and aft. O'Donovan rays at the ports. If Sorenson attacks *us* —"

He paused significantly. Zach Wheatley chuckled.

"Boy, you oughta see me whangle one of them rotor guns! I knocked the living be-Jupiter out of a rogue asteroid at four thousand on the way through the Belt."

"You said there were two reasons, Lieutenant," Plaice said, still curious. "The other?"

"Oh *that*!" Russ grinned. "It's about your latest stamp issue, Plaice. What in blazes have you been doing out here? You've got the P. O. in an uproar."

Plaice flushed. "There's nothing wrong with my issuing stamps," he said stiffly. "As postmaster of Iris, I have a government permit to do so. And I haven't been exceeding my issue allotment. I issue a five-cent, a ten, and a fifteen."

"Your five," said Russ, "is all right. So is your fifteen. But your ten —" He dipped a hand into his jacket pocket, brought forth a printed page torn from a book. "Get a load of this. It's a page from the newest Scott catalogue for stamp collectors. Check on your current ten-cent stamp, number thirteen-A."

The postmaster studied the philatelists' catalogue. Under each pictured postage stamp was a listing which gave a brief description of the stamp, along with its value in unused and used condition. This listing read:

IRIS MINERS' CONVENTION ISSUE, 2112

12. 5c yellow	12.00	35.00
13. 10c blue	24.00	60.00
13a. 1.0c violet	1000.00	3000.00
14. 15c sage green	60.00	1.45
14a. 15c dull green	75.00	1.80

Plaice gasped. "H-hey, that's not right! They must be crazy!"

"Of course it's not right," agreed Russ. "It looks as if you let one sheet get out in the wrong color. They're calling it the 'ten-cent error' back on Earth, and the stamp collectors are bidding their ears off for copies of it. By the time the next catalogue is issued, the value may have trebled. The Post Office Department is plenty sore about it, Plaice, They realize the value of new stamp issues. But if you're deliberately creating phony 'errors' to clean up —"

"Wait a minute!" interrupted Plaice hastily. "You don't understand. The whole thing's wrong! They've got the violet listed as the error. The *blue* is really the error."

"Ridiculous, Plaice!" Russ snorted. "Every kid collector on Earth has a copy of the blue. The violet is the freak. There are two copies known to exist in Io City, Jupiter. One copy is in Dr. Holswade's collection in the Ceres Museum."

"I'm not lying, I tell you!" stormed the bewildered postmaster. "I print those stamps myself. I grind the dyes and carve the engravings. It's a hobby, I guess. It gives me something to do when the mining is slow. But I tell you I never printed a ten-cent blue in my life!"

Russ studied the man thoughtfully. Either Plaice's sincerity was unquestionable or the man was a darned fine actor, and a liar to boot.

"There's something fishy somewhere, Plaice," he said slowly. "If you are right, these 'errors' are forgeries, and punishable as such. You know that, of course?"

"Naturally!" roared Plaice. He moved to his locker, began to scramble into his bulger. "Put on your space-suits, gentlemen. I'll show you my workshop right now."

"Bulgers in a building?" Zach Wheatley said. "Why?"

"Well," Plaice apologized, "the workshop's in a wing. An afterthought, and it's not altogether airtight. You don't exactly need a bulger, but it's better that way. It's warmer, and you don't get the ammonia fumes that creep in. Ready?"

He led the way to the workshop in which he prepared the postage stamp issues that were used for Iris franking and collected so eagerly by philatelists throughout the Solar System. Russ had only to glance at the equipment to see Plaice was telling the truth. But to clinch matters, Plaice opened a workbench drawer. He dragged forth several dozen sheets of gummed adhesives.

"See?" he said. "There's the current ten. Violet."

Russ nodded helplessly. He had often seen the supposedly normal ten-cent blue in friends' albums back home. The design of the stamp was the same — a crudely carved picture of a space ship jetting down to a space-weathered rock. The double inscription was in English and in the composite language, Universale.

"Iris Space Postage" was on one side. "Iris Eterro Postaj" was on the other. And beneath was the denomination, "10 cents."

Only the color differed from those copies Russ had seen. It was a bright violet, just as Plaice had claimed it should be.

"You win," said Russ. "But all I've got to say is, according to Earth standards and Scott's catalogue, you have here about two million bucks' worth of rare stamps!"

"Whoever faked them," raved Plaice, "whoever forged the copies made a blunder. Maybe they used an oxidized stamp as their guide. I don't know. Now, as to the fifteen-cent sage green, it is true that the color varies slightly. I've never been able to standardize it."

Zach Wheatley interrupted suddenly.

"You said you made your own dyes, Mr. Plaice. What do you use?"

"I don't see that it matters to you," began Plaice pettishly. Russ stopped him.

"Don't underestimate Zach, Plaice," he said quietly. "He's been around. For a hard-bitten old space-hound, he knows more about botany than any man I've ever met. He studies it just for fun."

"Oh!" Plaice coughed apologetically. "I'm sorry, Wheatley. This is all so upsetting." He frowned. "Now, let me see. I've been grinding my yellow from madder root. Alizarine, you know. The blue is natural indigo. And the violet is ground from the ordinary rock lichens that abound here."

"No anilines?" Zach said.

"Where would I get anilines? Iris is solid rock except for the scattered mineral deposits. There aren't any coal tar products nearer than Mars, though I did hear someone say traces of oil had been struck on Hebe." The superintendent-postmaster shrugged. "I tried to get the corporation supply ship to bring me some synthetic dye-stuffs, but they wouldn't. Said I was abusing company time, anyway."

Russ made up his mind suddenly.

"Let's go back to the office," he said. "I'm sure you're not responsible for the forgeries, Plaice. But there are a few unsettled points."

He separated the sheet of ten-cent stamps from the other, rolled them into a loose cylinder.

"What are you going to do, Lieutenant?" Plaice demanded.

"The only thing we can do. Take these back to Earth and put them on the market. The way I figure it, whoever printed those forgeries must have grabbed a monopoly on the *real* ten-cent violets. They flooded the market with the phonies and let a couple of the naturals sneak out to establish the 'error' and make it valuable.

"Now, undoubtedly, they'll try to capitalize on their trick. Sell the real stamps at a staggering over-valuation. But if I can get back to Earth soon enough, we'll spike their guns. We'll put these violets on the market at normal price."

"Well, I'm grateful to you, Lieutenant," Plaice sighed. "I'm doing the best I can out here. I don't want anyone to think I'm doing anything unethical."

They were back in the office now, removing their bulgers. Zach Wheatley had been pondering silently ever since he left the work ship.

"Mr. Plaice, did you say lichens?" he asked abruptly.

"What? Oh, yes. Ordinary lichens, ground into a pulp with water and a touch of potassium carbonate to hold it in solution."

"You got any of them lichens around here?" demanded Zach.

"Any?" Plaice snorted. "The rocks are covered with them." He turned to Russ. "Now let me have the mail, Lieutenant."

For the dozenth time since he had started this mail route among the planetoids, Russ experienced a heartwarming pleasure. He was helping Plaice distribute mail from home to the score of men who were Iris' inhabitants.

It was a simple thing, really. Plaice summoned the men from the mines. They came to the office one at a time, shuffling in their lead-booted bulgers, dirty and sheepish before the gaze of the trimly garbed SSP officer. But there was a touching eagerness in the way each took the slim bundle of envelopes bearing his own name.

Here was happiness on white paper, cased in a smooth, white folder. Here was new life and hope for them, a token that those on distant, scarce-remembered Earth still remembered them. Russ knew that in the three months' time that elapsed before the next mail ship arrived, these crisp envelopes he was now distributing would be dirty and frayed, worn with handling and numberless readings.

He wished he had three times as many letters for each man when he saw the way they fingered them, studied the return addresses, scanned the handwriting on the envelope, as if that also bore a message. He felt a pang of pity for the one man of the group who received no mail. He saw the swift flame of hope in the man's eyes die into shamed dullness. Russ made a mental note to see that the next mail would bring the disappointed one something, even if it were only a magazine or a letter from a Lonely Hearts club.

Then he collected their return mail, addressed to a dozen colonies throughout the Galaxy, but mainly to Earth. A slim note in Auld John MacAfee's crabbed handwriting was addressed to Miss Dorothy MacAfee. A half dozen letters from young Billy Barstow were addressed to as many different young ladies. One thick envelope came from Bud Mullins.

"Treat that one careful, Lootenant!" Mullins grinned cheerfully. "It's got all my wages in it for the past three months."

He went down the line, and at last it was time to go. Plaice was the last to contribute to the fattening mail pouch. From his safe he dragged four weighty packages. He hesitated a long minute before handing them over to Hodges.

"As the postmaster, Lieutenant," he said anxiously, "I should have no doubts. But as the superintendent and paymaster of the Corporation, I wonder if I should send this through with you? This is the refinement of our last three months' work. It's worth — well, plenty! Don't you think I ought to wait until the next trip?"

Russ laughed. "There'll never be a safer time to send it through than now. We're armed to the gills, and just hoping to see Sorenson's ship."

Plaice sighed and reluctantly handed it over. He bade his visitors farewell. But at the doorway, Zach Wheatley was still frowning. He turned for a last word.

"That there lichen," he said. "Was it orchil? Gray-like, and kind of fuzzy around the edges?"

"It was gray," said Plaice, "but I don't know what you mean by 'orchil'."

Russ was waiting impatiently at the air lock. Now he called out.

"Skip the botany lesson, Zach. We've got work to do. Come along!"

A few minutes later the *Spica* took off, zooming skyward on a belching tripod of flame. The next stop was Mars.

Russ Hodges yawned and looked at the chronometer on his instrument panel. The hands were rapidly closing on the figure twelve. He reached toward the call button, then drew back. Better to wait another minute. Sleep was too precious on these long drives to rob a comrade of a second of it.

But the door opened behind him. Zach Wheatley was already coming in to stand his trick at the board.

"Don't bother pushing, Russ," he said. "I'm here."

Russ yawned again.

"Good! I'm damn near dead. Trouble with these two-man flights is you never catch up on lost sleep. I've got a dead line on the Mars nineteen-point-oh-six orbit, Zach. Just hold to it."

"Are you telling me how to pilot?" Zach snorted.

"I couldn't tell you anything," Russ said lazily. "Not a thick-headed space-monkey like you. Well, see you later."

He went below. Wheatley hummed to himself as he glanced over the instrument panel. Direction, okay. Azimuth reading, okay. Shields up. Detection unit, check. He slid back his pressure chair, locked in the Iron Mike to hold her on course, and slouched across the room to the bookcase.

He was still worried about something. The worst of it was that he should know for sure. But he didn't. So he was going to look it up. He took down a book from the case, began pawing through the leaves.

Behind him, on the instrument panel, a small globe glowed red. Zach didn't notice it, for he was reading. As he read, his lips moved with the words and his head nodded understanding.

"*Lecanora tartarea,*" he said. "Sure, that's it! By golly, I —"

He darted eagerly for the panel. This discovery was important enough to warrant rousing the lieutenant from his slumbers. Zach's hand reached for the call button.

But he never reached it. At that instant there came a grinding shock, a crash that shivered hollowly through the *Spica*. In the space of seconds, even as Zach's horrified eyes sought the instrument panel and belatedly discovered the glowing, ruddy dot there, a tension beam had fastened to the mail ship. There were fumbling noises at the port, then the wheezing of the air-lock!

Scraping footsteps sounded below. Russ Hodges' head came popping up from the lower deck companionway like a startled hare from its warren.

"Zach!" yelled the still sleepy-eyed commander. "The air-lock! Somebody tied up to us!"

Zach was diving for the gun closet. He tugged at its stubborn handle, wrenched it open, reached for the hand ray.

"I wouldn't touch it if I were you, sailor," said a cool, derisive voice. Then the voice hardened, became curt and peremptory. "Stand back, both of you."

"Sorenson!" Russ Hodges yelled. "Balder Sorenson!"

The bulger-clad invader's lips twitched thinly. He flipped open the face port of his bulger, nodded to two men behind him to maintain guard. Then he tucked his own hand ray in its holster.

"Bless me, I get recognition. One becomes famous, doesn't one?"

Zach Wheatley growled, an animal sound that rumbled deep in his throat.

"One becomes a hunk of cold flesh!" he mimicked the space pirate's ponderous speech. "If one doesn't —"

"Zach!" said Hodges warningly.

Then, to Sorenson: "Well?"

"One does well," drawled the invader languidly, "to advise one's subordinates against discourtesy," Then again came that swift, characteristic change of mood, that snapping voice. "The mail, Lieutenant. Where is it?"

Russ Hodges' wrath darkened his face. His lips set grimly, stubbornly.

"Mail? I don't know what you're talking about."

Sorenson's hand fondled the butt of his ray gun.

"One does not like to use the term 'liar'," he said significantly. "But unless one receives a truthful reply, one has no choice."

Anger, despair, and bafflement created a chaotic fury in Lt. Hodges' mind. He cursed himself for having taken to his bunk while the *Spica* was in the raider's zone. He cursed Zach for having somehow permitted the enemy's speedster to approach within grappling distance of the mail ship.

But above all was his ire at what now seemed inevitable. He would have to turn over the mail to Sorenson, or both he and Zach might lose their lives and the mail would be forfeit anyhow. He made one final effort.

"I'm afraid you've made a mistake, Sorenson," he said. "This isn't a mail ship. The *Spica* is on special duty."

For a brief instant, Sorenson wavered. Hodges took heart when the bandit pursed his lips.

"Special duty, Lieutenant? One wonders exactly what this special duty might be?"

Russ realized, too late, that he had made a mistake which might prove fatal. In a vain attempt to protect his cargo, he had tipped his hand unwittingly. So far, Sorenson did not realize that the *Spica* was an armed fortress, specially prepared to destroy the pirate ship. His men had not stirred from the central control turret. But if his suspicions were aroused and he investigated the ship, he would discover the mounted rotor-guns and the *Spica's* miniature arsenal. Then it would be just too bad.

He thought swiftly, desperately. There must be a way out of this. And then, amazingly, Zach Wheatley was in motion. As he moved, he was shouting.

"Russ, get it out of your pocket! Swallow it. They'll never know!"

Russ stood numbed with bewilderment. But Zach made a scrambling dive toward Sorenson. It was a daredevil move, a reckless one. For a second, his life was balanced on the slightest pressure of the pirate's finger. But Sorenson did not shoot. Instead, he stepped aside nimbly and rammed his hand ray deep into Wheatley's side. To his men he purred:

"Watch this fool carefully!" Then he stalked to confront Russ, his eyes gleaming. "One judges there is something valuable in the lieutenant's pocket?" Deftly he shoved his free hand into Russ' jacket pocket. He took out the scrap of printed matter that was a page from the 2113 edition of the Scott catalogue. He stepped back, studying the sheet, perplexed.

"One needs enlightenment, Lieutenant," he admitted gently. "One does not quite understand."

Russ' face was fiery red. Was the whole world mad, or was he — or Zach? First Wheatley had allowed these marauders to gain possession of the *Spica*. Now he was making an insane uproar about a bunch of fake stamps.

"*You* don't understand?" he roared. "Well, neither do I, Sorenson."

"But one," persisted the invader thoughtfully, "is begin-

ning to understand. This rare postage stamp, the Iris ten-cent issue. One wonders if perhaps —"

Again it was Zach Wheatley's hoarse voice that took up the unfinished question. Almost sobbing, Zach cried out.

"Don't let him get them, Russ! They're worth more than two million bucks! He mustn't find them!"

"Two million dollars?" Balder Sorenson's pale eyes lighted. "One begins to understand your 'special duty,' my dear Lieutenant. One judges you have in your possession a number of these?"

Indignation had swept away all Russ' powers of deception. "Well?" he flared. "And what if I have?"

"Then," persisted Sorenson, "one would suggest that you turn them over. Immediately."

"But —" began Russ bitterly.

"One suggests that you spare us the 'buts.'"

Russ glared from one to the other of his accosters. Unexpectedly his eye met Zach Wheatley's. Zach stood quietly, covered by the ray guns of the two pirates, hands above his head. But there was a pleading look oh his face, a look that solidified into a tiny, almost imperceptible nod. Russ muttered, then shrugged.

"Very well. But I warn you, Sorenson, these things aren't like the cargoes you've been picking up."

Sorenson glanced once again at the scrap of catalogue in his hand.

"One knows quite well what they are, Lieutenant," he said. "One was a stamp-collector oneself, when one was young. And now, the stamps, please?"

And then Russ Hodges got it. He got it thoroughly, completely, for the first time. It took an effort to keep the inward smile from twitching his lips. But he was a pretty good actor. He continued to grumble as he strode to the turret room cabinet. He opened it and withdrew the small strongbox in which he had locked the Iris ten-cent stamps.

He flung open the lid. The sharp, keen bite of ammonia that had been imprisoned in the box with the adhesives cut the air. Russ tossed out the loosely rolled cylinder. "Well," he said grudgingly, "here they are."

Sorenson picked them up, bent over them swiftly, comparing them with the picture in the catalogue. He called one of his aides to his side.

"One is amazed!" he purred delightedly. "See, Todd? More than twenty full sheets of the ten-cent *violet*! A stamp error listed at a thousand dollars each." He chuckled again and slipped the valuable papers into his belt. "One feels this has been a successful raid, Lieutenant. Now one must be on about one's business. Ready, boys?"

Still covering the two SSP men, the invaders backed from the turret. As the door closed behind them, Russ made a dive for the gun closet. But Zach Wheatley was beside him, checking his move, "Wait, Russ! Let 'em get out, the dopes!"

They held their positions breathlessly until the chuffing

cough of the air-lock told them that the invaders had gone. Again there came that clanging of metal against metal, another tilting lurch of the *Spica* as the pirate ship loosed its tension beam. Then at last Zach Wheatley made a beeline for the starboard rotor gun. But this time it was Russ who attempted to stay his companion.

"No, Zach!" he yelled. "No! If they get away with those stamps, the error will be established for all time. Otherwise, it will mean a tremendous loss to the Department."

"Lemme alone!" yelled Zack. "I know what I'm doing, Russ!"

And he wrenched the concealing cover off the rotor gun. Not without reason had Zach Wheatley been called the finest gunner in space. Within seconds he had hairlined the rapidly accelerating pirate ship. He swung the gun to cover its line of trajectory.

His hand sought the lanyard, jerked. The *Spica* absorbed the reaction with a single, lurching wallow. There was no sound in the gun chamber.

But far away, the black dot which was the escaping pirate ship flared into a sudden, blinding flare. Cherry-red it glowed for an instant against the star-pointed ebony of space. Then a fiery needle of scotching gas writhed into nothingness where a moment before had been a ship, an escaped convict, and his marauding crew. Sorenson's day of terror was ended . . .

Afterward, Lieutenant Russ Hodges spoke soberly to his assistant.

"I guess I owe you an apology, Zach. But don't think it wasn't your fault that they boarded us in the first place. Considering the masterful way you tricked them into ignoring the mail cargo, though, I'll overlook that in my report." He chuckled, but not altogether mirthfully. "For a minute, I thought you'd gone space-batty. Then I caught on. By diverting Sorenson's attention to the stamps, you saved the rest of the stuff."

Zach Wheatley was a good sailor.

"Yeah, that's it, Russ," he said admiringly. "You're smart."

"But —" Hodges' face fell. "But it was too bad we had to blast their ship with the stamps in it. That's going to cost the Department plenty." He shook his head mournfully. "Two-million-bucks' worth of paper. *Blooie!*"

Wheatley grinned. "How much worth, Russ?"

"Two million. More or less."

"Mostly," said Zach, "less! Chief, do you want to see something funny?"

He led the way to the compartment in which the Iris mail had been stored.

He opened the canvas bag, lifted out, at random, the first letter he came to. It bore a ten-cent postage stamp. But as Lt. Hodges looked at that stamp, he gasped.

"Blue!" he cried. "A blue one, same as all the rest on Earth! But I don't understand, Zach. When that mail was stored, we know all the envelopes had the violet stamps on them!"

"That's right," said Zach cheerfully. "When they were stored. But they've been away from Iris for a couple of days now. Away from Iris' ammoniated atmosphere. They've been in the *Spica*'s air, which is like Earth's."

"I — I don't understand," said Russ.

"Neither did I, at first," admitted Zach. "But I felt like I ought to know. So I looked it up in some of my botany books. It's just a question of dye-stuffs."

"Dye-stuffs?"

"Yeah. Remember that Plaice told us he ground up his violet dyes out of lichens that grow on Iris? He said he pulped them with potassium carbonate. Well, it's a good way to make dyes. A swell way. Only the trouble is, them lichens he used was a variety known as *lecanora tartarea*. They use 'em on Earth for —"

"Yes?" said Russ.

"Litmus paper!" roared Zach gleefully. "That's why them stamps stayed purple on Jupiter and Io, but turned blue on Earth. That's why the stamps Sorenson stole ain't worth a damn! And that's why, when we get back to Earth, we can expose the 'ten cent error' as nothing but a freak."

Russ stared. Then he scratched his head. "Zach, this proves something," he said faintly. "But I don't know just what."

"I do," said Zach Wheatley cheerfully. "It proves that more chemists ought to be stamp collectors. Any one of them would have cleared up this mess in two shakes of a grasshopper's tail. And, say, talking about grasshoppers —"

"Yes?" said Lieutenant Hodges.

"One wonders," said Zach, "what the hell one did with one's chewing tobacco!"

THE TAPIR
by Arthur O. Friel

That is a queer thing, *senhores.* You say that the tapir, so common here in South America, is found in no other continent except Asia, and there only in a section which you call Malaysia; and that place is thousands of miles from our Brazil and across a vast ocean. How could our tapir have gotten there? He never could swim so far!

Oh, I see. Pardon my foolish question. Long ago there were tapirs all over the world, but now they have died out almost everywhere? Yes, I can believe that, for the tapir has no defense except his thick hide and his habit of jumping into water when attacked; and both animals and men must be able to defend themselves, or they will be wiped out by others which are more fierce and better armed. So perhaps the odd part of it is not that there are so few tapirs on earth now, but rather that there are any at all.

He is a shy fellow, the tapir. He needs to be, for he is hunted both by beasts and by men. Among the wild Indians of our jungle, as you perhaps know, the greatest hunter is he who can find and kill that big thick-skinned animal with funny nose. The prowling jaguar, too, is always eager to make a meal from him. Possibly you two North Americans also, during your explorations here at the Amazon headwaters, have slain a tapir or two for the sake of fresh meat. Yes? Then I need not tell you any more about that animal, for you probably know as much about him as I.

Still, I can tell you a tale of a tapir tonight, while this steamer slides along down the Amazon, which probably will amuse you. You have seen the tapir, observed his ways and tasted his flesh. But did you ever find one up in a tree, moaning and weeping from love?

Yes, it sounds ridiculous. But let me tell you, *senhores,* if ever I meet another love-sick tapir I shall go straight away and leave him, unless I am willing to get myself into trouble. And this is why.

One day in the flood season I was paddling down a swollen little river among wild hills in the Javary region — whether it was in Brazil or in Peru I do not know, for I had been on a long rambling trip into unknown country and neither knew nor cared where the boundary might be. With me was a fearless young comrade named Pedro, who, like myself, was a rubber-worker on the great, seringal of the Coronel Nunes. The floods having stopped our work in the swampy lowlands, we had taken a canoe and gone out to seek adventures — and had found them. And now, having used up nearly all our cartridges in a battle with head-hunting savages, we were on our way back to the headquarters of the coronel, paddling with our regular long distance stroke and expecting nothing at all to happen. But suddenly from the jungle near us came a mournful sound.

We held our paddles and looked. Only a few feet away was the hilly western shore of the stream, thick with bush. The sound had come from there, seeming to be a little distance away from the water and quite high up in the trees. We could not see anything in the tangle overhead, nor hear anything moving there. So after a minute I said softly to Pedro —

"Only a sick monkey grunting to himself."

He nodded slowly, as if in doubt, and continued squinting upward. I stroked again with my paddle, intending to go on. But before I put any power into the push the noise came again. I halted my arms.

"O-ho-o-o!" wailed a voice. "Oho-oo! Boo-hoo-hoo!"

We looked and listened. There was no sign of any man being in this place, but the voice was that of a man crying. It was a heavy voice, which ought to belong to a strong man; yet it was snuffling and sobbing there in the bush like that of a woman. To me, and I think also to Pedro, that sound was more dreadful than a cry of pain or a scream of fear; for it seemed that the man must be in a terrible condition to break down in that way. We turned the canoe, which had been drifting down the current, and silently paddled back.

Pedro, in the bow, jerked his head toward the shore. Looking closely, I saw what I had not noticed before — a quiet creek almost hidden by big drooping palm-leaves. We slipped the canoe through these leaves and stopped short. A few feet ahead of us was another canoe.

Then the voice came again. It was up over our heads.

"Oho-oo! What shall I do? I cannot live!" it sobbed.

More than twenty feet above the ground we spied a sort of house built in the branches of a big tree — a hut made from split palm logs and palm leaves. Up the trunk of the tree ran a stout notched pole making a ladder, such as we rubber-workers use in high tapping.

"The man must be dying alone up there, poor fellow," said Pedro.

I nodded. We stepped out on shore and went to the pole.

"What is the matter, friend?" Pedro called.

No answer came. There was a dead silence. Then we heard a slight movement up there, and out from a doorway at the top of the ladder came a head. We saw a dark face, with black hair and eyes. It peered down at us, and we started back. Then, without replying, the man swung himself out of the hut and came down the pole.

"*Por Deus!*" muttered Pedro. "He is not dying, nor even sick. He is as big and healthy as — as a tapir."

It was so. The fellow was so broad and heavy that it seemed as if the pole, stout though it was, ought to snap under him. Yet he was not clumsy; he came down so easily that we knew his muscles were strong and worked smoothly. I began to believe that there must be someone else up in that house, for it did not seem likely that this big man would have been moaning and blubbering so. But when he stood on the ground I saw that his eyes were wet and his face streaked, and the corners of his mouth turned down as if he were ready to start crying again.

As I looked at him I could not help grinning — partly because I was relieved, partly because his doleful face looked funny to me, and partly because Pedro's chance remark about a tapir was so near the truth. Above his heavy body and thick neck was the face of a tapir: for it was much narrower at the jaws than above the eyes, and the nose was so long and curving that it seemed to be not a nose but a snout. And, as I have said, the face was very dark, as the face of a tapir would be. He was a *caboclo*, with some white blood in him. Still, he looked like a good-natured young fellow, and he was not enough of an Indian to keep from showing his grief.

"What is the matter with you?" Pedro repeated. "We thought you were dying."

The other's mouth worked, and he sniffled.

"Maybe I am," he said in a choked tone. "I think I shall die. Oh, my poor little Bellie! Ah-hoo-wow!" He began to bawl.

"Your poor little belly?" demanded Pedro. "What ails your belly? It looks very healthy to me. Have you swallowed a live turtle?"

I snickered, and the tapir-man himself laughed. In the middle of a wail he changed his noise to a snort, and that in turn became heavy laughter. But then his mouth turned down again.

"You do not understand," he said. "I have lost my so-beautiful Bellie. It is a great misfortune, and not a thing to laugh about."

"Lost your appetite, do you mean?" asked my comrade. "That is nothing to make so much noise over. And I do not think your belly is so beautiful. It sticks out too much."

"No, no, you have it wrong!" the Tapir protested. "It is true I have no appetite — I have eaten nothing today, except some chibeh and a few handfuls of *pirarucu*-fish and some monkey-meat and a few other things. But that is because they have shut up my little Bellie for so long and will not let me have her. Even when they let her out I cannot have her — ah-hoo!"

"Stop that noise!" I ordered. "And stop your weeping also — it is wet enough here from the rains. Now tell us, what is this Bellie that gives you so much trouble? The matter must be serious if, as you say, you cannot eat more than two men need."

He nodded as quickly as his thick neck would let him, and told us:

"Indeed it is serious. My Bellie is a girl who has come to womanhood and should be given in marriage, but her father has not made ready for the feast, and so she is shut up. And the father does not favor me, but will give her to Gastoa. So you see it is a terrible misfortune."

"So I see," I said, "although I do not yet know just what you are talking about. Why is your girl shut up, and what has the feast to do with it? Tell us all about this matter. We are Pedro and Lourenço, *seringueiros* of Coronel Nunes. Perhaps we can help you."

He looked at us as if a little doubtful.

"I do not think you can help me," he said. "What I, Deodoro Maia, cannot do for myself is something no strangers can do for me. And perhaps even if we could free my Bellie I still should lose her. She likes men who are tall and handsome."

He looked at Pedro as he spoke. Pedro made a very low bow.

"Thank you, friend Deodoro," he laughed. "But have no fear. Girls do not interest me much. And if they did, I think perhaps I could get one without stealing her from another man."

Deodoro thought this over and nodded again.

"I think that is true," he admitted. After looking at both of us a while longer, he said: "Yes, I will tell you all about it. Will you come up into my house? I have some *cachassa*, but no tobacco."

"And we have tobacco but no *cachassa*," I replied. "It is a fair exchange — a smoke for a drink."

So I climbed the ladder and entered his house. He and Pedro followed.

It was dark inside the place, for it had only one small window-hole, its doorway was hardly big enough to let the tapir-man in, and the daylight outside was dull. Yet the hut was comfortable enough, and it was dry. When we were all inside Deodoro lifted a jug from a dim corner and passed it to us. After a good pull at the *cachassa* which it contained we sat down on the floor, with our backs to the wall, and tossed him the makings of a smoke. He could hardly wait to roll the cigarette before he lit it.

"Ah, that is good!" he grunted, sucking a huge drag of smoke down into his lungs and blowing it slowly out. "I have not had a smoke for days."

"That may be one reason why you have felt so badly," I told him. "It is a mistake to be without tobacco when you are in trouble. A drink and a smoke will go far toward easing any kind of pain."

"That is so," he agreed. "But I have been so miserable that I did not think of it. Besides, there is only one place where I can get tobacco — that is at the town; and Gastoa and his brothers and Bernardo, the father of my Bellie, drive me away from there."

We said nothing, but waited. Sitting in his big hammock, he puffed at the cigarette until it burned his fingers. The tobacco soothed him, as we knew it would; and with the smoke, another drink, and somebody to talk to, he became quite cheerful. Then he told us of his trouble.

He, Deodoro Maia, was a native of a small *caboclo* village some miles to the west, on another little river. The people of this town were jealous of their women and watched them closely. The young girls, who were only children, had nearly

as much freedom as the boys; but from the time when a girl reached womanhood until she was married she was watched continually — and after marriage too, for that matter. And it was the custom among these people, when a girl was old enough to take a man, for her parents to make a feast, and a celebration was held and everyone was told that the girl now could marry.

Now this custom, like many others, had both a good and a bad side. Whenever a girl grew up the whole village could have a merry time at the celebration. But the rule of having a feast at that time was so strong that unless the girls' parents were able to give that feast she could not be declared marriageable. In that case she was in a bad position; for she was no longer a child, with the child's freedom, nor yet a woman in the eyes of her people — she was nothing at all. Because of this, and also to keep her always guarded, her father would shut her up until he could give the usual feast.

This did not mean that she only had to stay in the house. A cage would be built — a tight, strong cage of woven cane inside the house — and she would be put into that cage and kept there like a beast. She might have to stay in that thing for many days; there was no escape for her until the feast was ready. Deodoro told us that sometimes a girl would be shut up so long that when she came out her copper-colored skin had faded almost to white.

Now Bernardo, father of the girl whom Deodoro wanted, was lazy and drunken, and meant to use his pretty daughter for his own benefit. So he intended to give her to a fellow named Gastoa, who was considered rich in his own village and had brothers who might help support the old drunkard in idleness; at least that was the father's plan. The man Gastoa was known to be cruel, and the girl feared and hated him; but that made no difference to old Bernardo, who thought only of an easy life for himself. He was so worthless, though, that when his girl-child turned into a woman he had nothing with which he could give the feast. Worse yet, he would not do enough hunting to get the monkey-meat usually dried and kept for the celebration. He only shut the girl into a cage and kept on drinking and sleeping.

So the moons came and went, and poor Bella — or Bellie, as the Tapir called her — was still a caged woman with no prospect of release.

The girl's mother did all she could for her. She worked hard to grow enough green foods for the feasting, and she tried to get Gastoa and his brothers to kill monkeys and salt away fish. But Gastoa was so sure he would have Bella in the end that he could not see any use in doing so much work for her, and so he and his family only laughed and sneered and did nothing.

And then a misfortune came to the crops. A herd of peccaries got into them and tore up almost everything, so that Bella's family had hardly enough left to live on, and all hope of the celebration was destroyed until new crops could grow.

When this happened Bernardo flew into a drunken rage. As might be expected, he vented his spleen on those who were not to blame. He beat his wife, and then he dragged his daughter out of her cage and beat her too because she was causing so much trouble to him. While he was still ugly Deodoro came in. A fight followed.

Deodoro, hoping to win the girl for himself, had done the thing which both Bernardo and Gastoa refused to do — he had hunted monkeys, birds, and fish, and dried or salted their meat. He had been very quiet about this, doing his work here at this house which he had built up in the tree, where nobody would be likely to find him. Now, with some of the best pieces of meat, he had gone back to the village to tell Bernardo he would give all he had toward the feast if he could have Bella for his own. But he came at a bad time, for, as I have said, Bernardo was ugly.

When he heard the young man's proposition he called him a vile name and kicked the meat into the dirt, where some dogs snatched it and ran off with it. Then he ordered Deodoro out; and when Deodoro hesitated he struck him. This was too much for even the slow, good-humored tapir-man to stand. He hit back and then started in to give the old fool the best thrashing of his life.

If he had been let alone he might have beaten some sense into Bernardo. But Bernardo, getting the worst of it, yelled for Gastoa to help him. Gastoa came, and his brothers with him, and jumped on Deodoro. They gave him such a beating that he was lucky to escape alive. Then they threw him out of the village, warning him not to come back.

In spite of this, Deodoro went back — though he took care not to go openly. Several times he went by moonlight, late at night when he knew the village was asleep. He even succeeded in talking a little with the girl through the thin cane wall of the house, and offered to cut a hole there and take her away with him. But, though she hated to be shut up so, still she wanted to be made a woman with the usual cere-mony, and she would not consent to running off to some unknown place where she could not see the people whom she had always known. Besides, she did not think very seri-ously of Deodoro. Nobody did, he said.

When we asked him why this was, he said it was partly be-cause of his white blood. He was neither a full-blooded *caboclo* nor a white man. His mother's father, he said, had been a white Brazilian trader who stayed for a time on that river while buying sarsaparilla for the market. Before his mother was born this man sailed away, and he never came back. So the girl was laughed at by the others because she had no father, and when she grew up she was sneered at be-cause she was half white. In the same way her son Deodoro was laughed at in his turn, though his own father was a *caboclo*. The only one who did not jeer at him, he said, was the girl Bella, who sympathized with him when the rest

mocked him.

This story made us sorry and angry — sorry for the young fellow and angry at those who had treated him so. We saw that he was not by nature a fighter, and that, with the whole town against him and the girl unwilling, he felt that there was nothing he could do but stay in his tree and be miser-able. He was much in need of help.

"The big question is, does the girl care for you?" said Pedro. "Does she want you more than another?"

Deodoro stared out of the door awhile before he an-swered.

"I do not know just what she wants," he said then. "I do not think she knows either. She has not seemed to think much about men. I know she likes me as well as anyone, and much better than she likes Gastoa. She does not like him at all."

"She likes you but she does not admire you," said Pedro. "Then you have two things to do — to free her and to make her respect you. Women admire men who are strong and bold. Be strong and bold, friend, and she will realize that you are a man. Now she thinks of you as a boy. Am I right?"

The Tapir thought again and agreed.

"You have it right," he said. "But what can I do? I can not go into the town and shoot everybody that tries to stop me from taking her away. My bullets are all gone."

We laughed.

"Of course you can not," said Pedro. "That would be a blundering way. Even if you shot down the whole town you would not win what you want most — the girl herself. She would then fear you more than she fears Gastoa. You want her to admire you, not to be afraid of you. Now let us try to make a plan."

So we talked about different ideas that came to us, but none of them got us anywhere. At length I said:

"We are wasting time. You and I, Pedro, have never been at this place where Deodoro lived, and all we know about it is what he tells us. We might sit here and talk for a week, and then go there and have our great idea smashed by some little thing none of us had thought of. The one thing we are sure about is that first the girl must be gotten out of her cage. The best way to get that done is to go ahead and do it."

Deodoro nodded seriously, as if I had said a very wise thing. Pedro laughed, but he agreed.

"That is the best plan of all," he said. "Let us go with God and trust to luck."

We arose and turned toward the door. But Deodoro halted us.

"Wait," he said. "I am feeling much better, and I think I can eat something before we start. I have all the meat I saved for the feast — except the few pieces I lost at Bernardo's house — and now I shall not give any of it to those who have not treated me well, but will keep it for myself and Bellie and my friends Pedro and Lourenço. I think we had better have some of it now."

"You have spoken most wisely, friend," Pedro answered with a grin. "My comrade and I have not been eating much for the last few days. We have been on a long trip and our supplies are nearly gone. So we shall not throw your meat to the dogs as Bernardo did. But where do you keep it?"

"Since you are my friends, I will show you," he replied with a sly look.

Lifting a couple of the split palms that made his floor, he brought out meat.

"See, my floor is double," he explained. "The big branches of this tree hold up my house, and between the branches I have made boxes, and then covered branches and all with my floor. It is a good way to hide things."

"Deodoro, you are one of the cleverest fellows I ever met," said Pedro. "Few men would have thought of such a thing."

Deodoro's face beamed. Probably it was the first time anybody had ever praised him; and somehow he seemed to grow bigger as he thought about it. Pedro gave me a slight wink, and I saw what he was trying to do — to make this shy, downcast fellow think well of himself. And indeed, *senhores*, that is a thing that has much power to help or harm a man; for if he does not feel himself to be the equal of other men, who else will believe him to be so? Seeing Pedro's thought and realizing its value, I changed my own manner toward the young tapir-man and no longer treated him as a boy.

We went down the pole, built a little fire and ate. Pedro and I were hungry, and we did not spare the meat; but I do not believe that both of us together ate as much as Deodoro put away alone. When the food was gone he was still hungry, and he climbed the ladder and brought down more. This time he brought down his jug also. We found that it held more *cachassa* than we had thought, but we emptied it. Then, feeling quite merry, we got into our canoes and pushed out into the river.

With our new comrade leading, we paddled downstream until he swerved to the left. Up another quiet creek we followed him. The stream widened into a long swampy lake which seemed to have no end, for it wound along among the low hills so that whenever we thought we had reached the end we found that there was more of it. At length, when we had about concluded that it was no lake but a flooded arm of the river ahead, Deodoro led us into another narrow stream. Down this we went, and soon we came out into another river.

"It is not far now," said Deodoro in a low tone. "It is only a short paddle upstream."

"Very good," Pedro replied. "But why do you speak so quietly? You are not afraid if the whole world hears you."

Again Deodoro seemed to swell.

"No!" he agreed, and his heavy voice boomed like a gun. "I do not fear any man!"

He began paddling again with a bold stroke.

As he said, it was not far to the town. We heard it before we saw it. Shouts and laughter came to us, and then someone began to beat a drum in Indian time. Deodoro suddenly stopped paddling.

"There is a celebration," he said. "I wonder — it can not be — it is not possible that Bernardo has made the feast!"

"If there is a feast, so much the better," I said. "Everyone will get drunk. Is it not so?"

He nodded.

"Then it will be easier for us to do what we come for," I explained. "When all are drunk, who shall stop us?"

He made no answer. We saw that he was worried, thinking the noise might mean that his girl was given to the man Gastoa.

"Come, comrade," said Pedro. "We are stopping here as if we were afraid."

The hint was enough. Deodoro's head came up, and he swung into his stroke as if he owned the river. Pedro let out a yell, and we joined in. Shouting and paddling hard, we surged up to the town like men sure of a welcome.

Like all towns in that region, it was on a hill above the reach of any floods. In the dry time it probably was some distance from the stream, but now the high water made it easy for boatmen to land beside it. As we stepped out on shore the drum-beating stopped. Several men came to meet us, and some barking dogs rushed at us.

Pedro knocked the dogs aside with his rifle. I had no gun, for I had broken mine and lost it in that fight with the headhunters of which I have told you. But I had two good feet in heavy boots, and I used them. One of the dogs, an ugly brute, snarled as if about to spring at me, but I kicked him again so hard that he yelped and retreated. At this, one of the men scowled at me in evil fashion.

"Kick my dog again and you will get yourself into trouble," he growled.

"I am used to trouble," I retorted. "And I kick an ugly dog wherever I meet him — whether he stands on four legs or on two."

He glared and took a step toward me. Then he halted as if not quite sure of himself. After glowering at me for a minute he shifted his gaze to Deodoro.

"You Deodoro!" he snarled. "Did I not tell you not to come back here?"

"You did, Gastoa," answered the tapir-man. "But you see I am back. I think I shall stay, too." His voice was strong and steady.

Three other men scowled when they heard this. I judged that they were the brothers of Gastoa, who had helped to beat Deodoro and drive him out. More *caboclos* had gathered around us now, and among them I noticed a short, piggish-looking man of middle age who seemed quite drunk. Pointing at Deodoro, this man yelled:

"Throw that one into the river! Throw the others in! Drown them all! What business have they here?"

Gastoa and his brothers growled again, but they did not quite dare to rush us. We stood shoulder to shoulder, and they could easily see that we did not intend to be driven away without a fight. Before they could decide just what to do Pedro spoke.

"Is your name Bernardo?" he asked.

The drunken man blinked at him.

"Yes, I am Bernardo."

"I thought so," said Pedro. "I had heard that in this town lived a man named Bernardo who was a know-nothing and a drunkard. I knew you must be the one, because nobody but a drunken fool would try to drown strangers who came to trade and make his town rich."

Bernardo became furious. He screeched that Pedro lied. But the other men looked at us with a new expression in their faces. Then one of them roughly told Bernardo to be quiet; and when he kept on yelling two others shoved him away. By this time everyone in the place was there at the shore. They all stood staring, and I saw some whispering to one another.

"Is that the truth?" demanded Gastoa. "Have you come to trade?"

"You do not think we came to look at your handsome face, do you?" sneered Pedro. "Who is the head man here? I will do my business with him."

The crowd opened, and out stepped a man who was rather old but looked strong and shrewd.

"I am chief," he said. "I, Araujo."

His sharp eyes went to our canoe, which now held only the few supplies that remained after our long trip.

"If you come to trade, where are your trade goods?" he asked.

"Greetings to you, *compadre*," said Pedro, as if the head man were no better than the rest. "Surely you do not think we would bring our goods in that little canoe. It will take a big *batelao* to carry the things we have for you — that is, if we decide to trade with you. This is not a small matter of wax and salt fish."

His insolent manner made Araujo frown, but I could see that he and all the rest were impressed by it and by his big talk. I had no idea of what tale Pedro intended to tell, but I saw he had made a good beginning; so I tried to look like an important trader, instead of what I was — a bush-tramp with hardly enough food and cartridges to get home on. The thought came to me that Deodoro might show surprise and betray us. But a glance at him showed me he had more sense than that. His face was like wood, and he was looking straight ahead.

"What do you want for this *batelao* full of riches?" asked the head man.

"We will talk alone with you about that," Pedro told him.

"We do not do our business on the riverbank. And before we do any business at all we want food for ourselves and this guide of ours, Deodoro."

Araujo looked as all over again, staring hard at Deodoro, who stared back at him. Then he nodded and turned away. We followed him, and I noticed that the crowd now was looking in friendly fashion at our Tapir companion and sourly at Gastoa. The reason was easy to see; they believed Deodoro had brought us there to make them rich, and that Gastoa had angered us and might have lost them their chance to trade. I had hard work to keep from grinning.

"You have come in time to eat at the feast," said Araujo. "This is a feast-day here. A girl has come to womanhood."

"What girl?" asked the Tapir.

"Not the one you are thinking of," the old man answered. "It is the youngest daughter of Fontoura."

"Oho! So you have a girl here, Deodoro!" teased Pedro, as if he had not heard of it. "You sly fellow, why did you not tell us?"

Deodoro looked queerly at him, but made no answer. The head man chuckled.

"There are several men between him and his girl," he explained. "And the girl has not yet been made a woman. So I would not say that he has any."

We had gotten away from the crowd by this time, and he stopped.

"Now you can tell me your business," he said.

"*Amanha* — tomorrow," Pedro answered, "I never do business on a feast-day; and since we have been lucky enough to come at a time of merry-making, we will join you in it. Tomorrow, when I have rested, we can talk of this matter."

Araujo scowled again. So Pedro added —

"Today it is enough to ask you whether you can get sarsaparilla roots, and perhaps Peruvian bark, for us from the forest near here."

The face of the chief brightened.

"Yes, yes! There is much in the hills above here."

"Then our guide has not lied to us," said Pedro, as if well pleased. "Perhaps you have heard of the big new company of Englishmen who now are working out of Tabatinga and preparing to buy these medical things for the markets in Europe?"

Araujo had not. Neither had I, and neither had Pedro. But the chief now thought he understood.

"And you are the scouts of this company," he guessed. "You are very welcome. We can make much trade for you. What do you give for those roots?"

But Pedro shook his head.

"*Amanha*," he said again.

So, seeing that he would talk no more of business that day, Araujo told us the town was ours.

The drum started up again, and others joined in. Men

came to us with liquor and meat, and we ate and drank well — for we had paddled several miles since eating at Deodoro's tree-hut, and our appetites again were strong. Everyone made us welcome — that is, all but Bernardo and Gastoa and his gang. They stayed by themselves, talking angrily and drinking much.

I was glad to see that they drank, for I felt that they were the ones whom we needed to watch most, and hoped that in the end they would make themselves senseless. If we waited until night, I thought, it should be quite easy to get the girl out of her prison and escape with her. But Deodoro spoiled that plan.

Before long the *caboclos* formed for a dance around the drummers. It was not much of a dance. They only trotted around and around, yelling and laughing, and dropping out one by one for a drink now and then. Araujo, the chief, trotted with the rest, tooting solemnly on a little tin whistle he had gotten somewhere. Some of the men shouted to us to join in, and I saw several young women making eyes at Pedro; but we said we were tired and squatted by ourselves, smoking and watching. Then Pedro said to Deodoro:

"Now is a good time for you, comrade, to slip away and talk to your girl. She must feel very badly at hearing all this merriment, knowing that it is for another girl, while she remains cooped up. She ought to be ready to run away with you now. If she is, tell her that at the right time we will take her where she can be happy."

The young fellow started to rise. Pedro grabbed him and pulled him down.

"Not like that!" he cautioned. "Do not get up and walk away in plain sight. Creep around behind us and then crawl behind this house at our backs. After that you can walk."

The big fellow grunted and obeyed. Like the tapir he resembled, he was not very good at creeping. He made some noise as he went. But nobody seemed to notice his going. Between the liquor and the dancing, the *caboclos* now were getting quite drunk and thinking of nothing but their own fun. So our companion got away without being seen.

We sat for a while longer watching the circling crowd. Then Pedro said:

"They are a worthless lot, Lourenço. Even if we were the traders they think us to be I doubt if I should want to do business with them. They look lazy, mean and treacherous. They have no welcome to a stranger unless they hope to make something from him, and their laughter now is only the kind born of drink and drums. I shall be glad when we are out of this place. This is the first time I ever took a hand in a woman-stealing."

"That is the way I feel too," I agreed. "I am not afraid of them, but I dislike them all. And unless Deodoro's girl is better than the women I have seen here she is hardly worth our time and trouble."

"He thinks she is," he laughed. "And every man must be

his own judge in such matters. But I wish he would come back. I want to get up and walk around — those drums make me restless. If we do that, though, the *caboclos* will notice that he is gone."

It did seem that Deodoro had been gone for some time, and as the throbbing of the drums went on I too wished I could move around. A few minutes later I was moving around more than I had expected to.

A yell broke out. The dancers stopped. We hopped up. Then, before a house near the water, we saw men fighting and a girl running toward the stream.

"The fool!" snorted Pedro. "He has let her out too soon!"

We ran toward the struggle. So did everyone else. One of the fighting men broke away and dashed after the girl. Another fell backward and lay still. But there were four of them left, and three of them were attacking Deodoro. They were Gastoa and two of his brothers. The man on the ground was the third brother.

As we reached them, Gastoa himself went down. The Tapir was fighting only with his hands, but those hands were terrible enough.

He got a clumsy swing into Gastoa's face, and it cracked like flat wood hitting water. Gastoa fell like a dead man. After he was down I caught a glimpse of his face. It looked as if a real tapir had jumped on it — mashed flat.

Pedro and I knocked down the other two men and yelled to Deodoro to run. All three of us jumped for our canoes. We ran into the girl and the man who had seized her. She was screaming and trying to escape. The man was her father, and he was striking her brutally in the face and body.

Pedro, the quickest of us three, reached them first. He jolted Bernardo in the head with his rifle-butt, and the drunkard fell sprawling. Without a pause Pedro snatched the girl off the ground and kept on running. But the crowd was almost on us, and as we slowed at the water's edge they caught us.

"Go!" I grunted to Pedro. Then I yanked his gun from his fist, whirled and struck around me. Men fell, but others swarmed in. I heard grunts and blows beside me and knew somebody was helping me to fight, but I had no time to see who it was. I thought it must be Pedro. Later I was surprised to find that it was Deodoro.

Pedro had hastily pushed the girl into our canoe and then turned back. But Deodoro, thinking only of getting the girl away, shoved Pedro backward so that he tumbled into the canoe, and then he heaved the boat out into the river. In falling, Pedro hit his head hard against the bottom of the canoe, and the blow stunned him so that he lay there a few minutes while he and the girl drifted away downstream. Then the fighting Tapir wheeled back to help me hold off the furious crowd.

Between us we did some rough work. But we were outnumbered; and to tell truth, *senhores*, I never got such a beating in my life. I have fought hard before and since that time, and have had far more serious wounds than I received then; but those *caboclos* knew how to hit where it would hurt. If they had had their weapons they would have cut me to pieces. But none of them had stopped to pick up a knife, and now they could fight only with hands, feet and teeth. Those were enough.

Somehow I did not think of shooting. I could not have shot well if I had tried, for they were too close. They wrenched at the gun while they beat me, and how I kept it I do not know. But I did keep it, and slugged around me with muzzle and butt. Finally, though, they knocked my legs out from under me. I fell hard, and they jumped all over me.

I kicked and squirmed and bit, but they had me. Then suddenly I felt a tremendous tug at one foot. I went sliding and bumping down the bank with two men hanging to me. Blows sounded and the men fell away. Somebody tumbled me head first into a canoe. The canoe slid outward.

A raging yell sounded behind me. Sitting up, I found myself afloat. With me was the Tapir. His face was battered and his big snout was gushing red, but he was as strong as ever. He had grabbed a paddle and was shoving the boat downstream with strokes so powerful that the dugout seemed to leap from the water. As I looked at him he grinned through split lips.

"I had to pull hard to get you out of that tangle," he said. "You seemed stuck to the ground."

I tried to answer, but all I could do was to make a wheezing sound. The wind was beaten out of me. So I sat still while my breath came back and my head grew clear. I saw that the *caboclos* were jumping into boats and coming after us. Then we caught up with my own canoe, where the girl was crouching and Pedro was getting up and reaching for a paddle. Pedro had a surprised look, as if wondering how he had come there, but he wasted no time in talk. Scooping up a handful of water, he threw it on his head and then began to paddle hard.

I looked for a paddle too, but there was none. Deodoro was using the only one in this canoe. I still had the rifle, though; and, seeing that the maddened men behind were gaining on us, I began shooting. I did not shoot to kill, for I do not like to kill men if it can be avoided. At the same time, I shot close enough to make them think I meant death.

Aiming carefully, I sent several bullets thumping along the sides of their dugouts. They slowed up at once. Some yelled to stop, others shouted to go on, and they paddled both ways at once — some trying to keep after us and others backing water. While this was going on we drew away fast.

The Tapir swerved into the bank and up the same stream we had traveled before. Pedro followed. For some time we kept on at the same rate of speed, and then we came out into the long crooked lake. There we stopped, listened — and heard nothing.

"They have given up," panted Pedro.

The Tapir shook his head.

"They have gone back for guns, and they follow," he said. "But we can dodge them. There is more than one way out of this lake."

Looking around as if to get his bearings, he pushed on again. Down around a bushy point we went, and there turned sharp to the right. A short arm of water ran that way, and we traveled down this until we seemed about to bump the shore. Then he swung to the left, and we were in a quiet, winding stream. There we stopped.

I got up with grunts and groans, for I had been sitting still and my bruised muscles had stiffened so that each one had a pain of its own. Deodoro grinned again. The grin annoyed me.

"Now," I demanded, "tell me why you got us into all this trouble. Why did you not come back to us and wait until we were ready?"

"You said yourself that the first thing to do was to free Bellie, and that the quickest way to free her was to go ahead and do it," he answered. "So I went and did it. And your comrade Pedro told me to be strong and bold. Have I not been strong and bold?"

His face and voice were so serious that Pedro and I laughed.

"More bold than we wanted you to be," I told him.

"I am sorry you got hurt," he said. "But I went and talked to Bellie and found her mad to get out at once. So I thought I had better take her before she changed her mind, and I cut a hole and pulled her through. If Gastoa and his brothers had not sneaked up just then we should have gotten away without trouble. And nobody would have thought you two traders had anything to do with it, because you were sitting in plain sight all the time."

"I see," I said. "And now that we are all here I think you had better take your girl and let me get into my own canoe."

We had been holding to bushes while we talked, and now Pedro drew our canoe up beside me. For the first time I had a good look at the girl, and after that look I did not blame Deodoro for wanting her. She was very pretty. True, she looked thin and weak, and her skin seemed pale; but I remembered that she had been caged for a long time, and knew that a healthy life outdoors and plenty to eat would quickly make her plump and strong. Her eyes and mouth were beautiful, and she looked no more like the other women we had seen than a butterfly looks like a mud-worm. Remembering the evil face of Gastoa and the brutality of her father, I was glad I had gone to help her, even though I now was full of aches and pains.

Then I noticed something that was not so pleasing. She did not want to leave Pedro and come to Deodoro. She looked long at Pedro, then glanced at the tapir-man and wrinkled her nose. I too looked at both the men, and saw what a difference there was. Pedro was a graceful fellow, with merry brown eyes and curly hair; and he had not been hit during the fight, so his face was not marked at all. Deodoro, with his clumsy-looking body and lank hair and big nose, was not a beauty at any time; and now his eyes were swollen so that they peered through slits, and his whole face was bruised and bloody.

It came to me, too, that though Deodoro had given the girl her chance to escape from the house, it was Pedro who had attacked Bernardo when she was being beaten and had run with her in his arms to the water; so that she might easily feel that it was the handsome stranger who had saved her. Besides, she had not seen Deodoro's one fight at the house, because then she was running for the river. And she probably did not know much about his battle on the bank, for then she was floating away and we were all tangled up in a lighting knot. Poor Deodoro! Everything seemed to be against him.

Whether he saw all this I did not know, but I hoped not. When the girl made no move to change canoes I spoke gruffly to her, telling her to make room for me. She rose then though slowly, and took my place without a word.

As I settled down and picked up my paddle I heard voices out on the lake. We slipped the canoes silently downstream and looked. The Tapir was right — two boatloads of armed *caboclos* were passing, the men working hard and looking ahead. Others came behind them. We kept very quiet until they were gone.

"They will go down the lake to the end hunting us," said the Tapir. "Then they will work back and search all the coves. We shall be at my house long before they have finished here. Are you not glad to be free, Bellie?"

The girl made no answer. Her eyes came again to Pedro's face, and then she looked down into the water. Deodoro looked long at her, then at Pedro, then at me. His face grew sad. With a deep sigh he pushed his canoe against the slow current, and we passed silently up the creek.

After a time we came into a network of winding water courses without any current that I could see. Deodoro hesitated several times, but seemed always to pick the right one. At length we found ourselves again in flowing water, and now we went downstream instead of up. At length we entered the river on which Pedro and I had been traveling that morning.

There our leader turned downward, and we saw that he had brought us out above his house. Keeping near the left shore and watching sharply for *caboclos*, we soon reached the little inlet masked by the palms.

"Now you are safe, Bella," I said when we stepped out on shore. "See the fine house Deodoro has built for you up here in the tree, where you can always be dry and comfortable. It is much better than any house in your town, and you will never have to live in a cage again. He has much meat too,

and you and he will have plenty to eat. You will be very happy here."

"Do you two stay here also?" she asked.

"No," I said. "This is Deodoro's place. We must go on, for we live far from here."

She glanced once more at the house in the tree. Then she cried:

"I do not want to stay here, I will not stay here! Take me away!"

We all stood silent, staring at her. I wanted to scold her, but knew that would do no good. So I said the first thing that seemed best.

"We cannot take you away today, Bella — it will soon be night. And we two are not going until tomorrow. We shall rest and eat here. Tomorrow we shall see what is best to be done. Now go up and see what a fine house that is."

She stood still, stubbornly, until Pedro also told her to mount the ladder. Then she obeyed, climbing as if afraid she would fall, but going upward until she got into the hut.

"*Nossa Senhora!*" muttered Pedro. "Now this is a pretty mess! After all our trouble she wants to go back home."

Slowly the Tapir shook his head. His face was full of pain.

"No, it is not that," he said. "It is as I told you before we went. She likes tall handsome men, and I am not tall nor handsome."

He swallowed hard, as if trying to keep from crying. And then, through his teeth, he added:

"She wants to — to go with you, Pedro. If she will — be happier with you, comrade, then — then you had better take her with you."

He choked and turned away.

For an instant Pedro stared. Then he sprang and caught him by the shoulder.

"*Par Deus*, you are a man!" he said. "Why, comrade, I do not want your girl! I do not want any girl at all. And you are wrong — she does not want me either. She may be interested in me because I am a new man whom she has not seen before, but after I am gone she will quickly forget me."

But Deodoro shook his head again, and so did I. I had seen women fall swiftly in love with Pedro before this — women who knew more about men than this little girl-woman knew; and I felt that Bella would not forget him so quickly as he said, and that neither she nor Deodoro would be happy because of this. When Pedro asked me if I did not agree with him, I said no.

"There is some truth in what Deodoro says," I told him, "If she had not seen you she might have been happy with him. I think our work is only half-done. We have freed her, but how are we to make her satisfied?"

He scowled and stood thinking. Then his eyes began to twinkle, and he threw up his head and laughed.

"Deodoro, let me talk to you," he said. "Lourenço, climb

up and talk with her so that she will not overhear us. Ask her if she would like to go away with me — but try to show her that she would be foolish to do such a thing."

I did as he said. Up the pole I went, and in the hammock I found the girl, looking very small and sad and dissatisfied. When I came in she brightened up and glanced beyond me as if expecting someone else. Seeing that nobody followed, she seemed disappointed.

"The others will be up soon," I informed her.

Then I sat down against the wall, grunting from the pain of my stiff muscles.

"I am very lame," I went on. "Still, I am glad I am alive to feel lame. If it had not been for the splendid fighting of Deodoro I should probably be dead — and you would be back in your cage, to be beaten by your father and given to Gastoa."

She turned more pale at that thought, but looked surprised too. And she asked what Deodoro had done that was so brave. So I saw that I was right — she did not realize what a fight he had made. Taking care not to praise him over-much, I told her how he had fought off the gang of Gastoa and then battled beside me so that she could get away, and how he had pulled me out when I was down. Her big dark eyes grew larger as I talked.

Then, when her mind was full of this new fighting Deodoro, I suddenly asked her whether she would like to go away with us.

"My friend Pedro likes you," I said, "and if you want to go with him we can fool Deodoro in some way. You might not be happy with Pedro, but —"

"Why not?" she cut in.

"Well, of course he is a handsome man," I pointed out, "and other girls like him very well, and you could not expect him to give all his time to you. He would not stay with you as this simple Deodoro would do. And he likes his fun with men too, and so he would drink and gamble with them. And he is restless and will not stay long in one place — and you know he would not want you trailing after him everywhere. If you expected him to be as faithful to you as Deodoro would be, you might not be happy. But if you are willing to be reasonable about those things we can take you away when we go. He is keeping Deodoro down below while I ask you about this."

Senhores, that gave her a good deal to think about. At first she looked as if she wanted to cry, and I felt sorry for her — but I did not let her see that. Then, she asked the question I expected.

"If he wants me, why does he not talk to me himself instead of sending you?"

I laughed as if that were a foolish question.

"Because Deodoro would probably fight to keep you, and Pedro knows how hard he would fight. Pedro probably would get his handsome face hurt. And besides, what is the

sense of fighting over a woman? Deodoro thinks you are the only pretty woman in the world, but Pedro and I know you are not."

She looked at me then as if beginning to dislike me. Before we could talk more we heard Pedro's voice down below, and it was loud and ugly.

"Then if you have more *cachassa*, why did you not say so?" he demanded. "I want a drink and I want it now! After we have gone to that dirty town of yours and brought back that female for you, I call it shabby treatment to try to hide your liquor!"

"You can have a drink if you want it," came the voice of the Tapir. "But do not speak so of my girl. She is not the kind of girl that a man like you ought to talk about."

"Bah! The world is full of girls, and not one of them is worth anything. I want that drink!"

"Then come up and you shall have it."

I stuck my head out of the door beside me and looked down. Deodoro, I noticed, had washed his face and looked much better. As he came upward and saw me he grinned. Pedro, behind him, winked at me. But when they came into the house their expressions had changed. Deodoro looked very serious, and Pedro scowled.

The Tapir lifted part of his floor again, and this time he pulled up a jar which he handed Pedro. My partner seemed to take a huge drink. When he passed the jar to me, however, I found that very little of the liquor was gone. I took as much as I wanted, and then held it out toward Deodoro. But Pedro snatched it and appeared to swallow about half of what was left, making a guzzling noise and letting some of the cachassa drip off his chin. The girl watched all this, and a look of disgust crept across her face. The thought came to me that my comrade's actions must remind her of her drunken, worthless father.

Then Pedro slumped down beside me and rolled a cigarette. Usually he was very deft at making a smoke, but now his fingers seemed clumsy. He spilled most of his tobacco, and then he snarled. He tried again, and made a worse mess than before. Finally he ordered me to make his cigarette for him. I did so, but I took my time about it. Then he abused me because I was so slow, and growled once more at Deodoro because he had not been more free with his liquor. After the cigarette was lit and going well, though, he quieted somewhat.

None of us spoke while he smoked, Deodoro watched us solemnly, and I saw the girl studying him and Pedro in turn. Pedro's face grew more heavy, as if the *cachassa* were working on him. Presently he began to leer at Bella.

"Think I will take you downriver with me, girl," he said roughly. "You do not want to stay here and you do not want to go back to your cage. You have to go somewhere, so come with me."

She looked him straight in the eyes. Then she said —

"I do not think I want to go with you."

"What!" snapped Pedro. "Do not be a little fool!" He looked at Deodoro and grinned in a nasty way, as if the liquor had given him courage which he had lacked before. "You, Deodoro, you can stay here with your *cachassa*. I am going away with this woman of yours. I am going now!"

He lurched up and staggered toward the girl.

Then the Tapir moved. He swooped at the rifle Pedro had left leaning against the wall. He jammed the muzzle into my comrade's stomach, and I heard the hammer click back.

"Stop where you are!" he ordered. "You shall not take her away. She is too good for you."

Pedro stood very still, staring down at the gun as if stricken with fear. I got up as quickly as I could, drawing my machete, for I did not like the sound of that hammer going back. But before I could get within arm's length of Deodoro the girl jumped at me.

She came so suddenly and swiftly that before I realized it she had knocked my bush-knife from my hands. With another lightning move she threw it out of the door, and I heard it thump on the ground below. Then, her face full of fury, she warned me —

"Keep back or I will tear your eyes out!"

I kept back. Her nails were very long, and I had seen how quick she was. Her sudden action had taken us all by surprize, and we stood staring at her. Then Deodoro spoke again to Pedro.

"If she wished to go with you and if you would be kind to her I would let her go. But I know you have other women. You boasted about it when you first came here and drank my cachassa. You said you only played with women, and that when you tired of one you left her and got another. You will not do so with Bellie."

Pedro made no answer. He looked at Bella. She looked back, at him as if now she hated him. To Deodoro she said:

"You are the only honest man I know, Deodoro. I will stay with you and be your good girl. Drive these two into the river! This one is no better than the other." She pointed at me. "He wanted me to fool you and run away with them. Drive them out!"

"Get down the pole!" grunted the Tapir savagely. "Bellie, stay here!"

Pedro glanced at me and jerked his head toward the door. We went down the pole, Deodoro still covering us.

"Do not touch that machete!" he warned, as I stepped toward my knife. "Go to your canoe."

"Come, Lourenço," whispered Pedro. "He will follow."

So we got into our canoe. Deodoro came down, picked up my weapon and. stepped into his own boat.

"Out into the river!" he commanded.

Pedro, looking much afraid, splashed his paddle quickly into the water and we moved outward. Behind us came the Tapir.

As we went downstream I felt the canoe shaking. I could not understand this until I looked at Pedro.

The drunken look was gone from his face, and, though he made no sound, he was laughing so hard that he could scarcely use his paddle.

"Over to the right, where you see that *massaranduba* tree," came the voice of the Tapir.

We turned to the place. Below the tree we found a little cove which twisted around like a hook. At its end, where it could not be seen from the river, was a small hut.

There we got out. Pedro leaned on his paddle and laughed again. The Tapir, grinning, handed us our weapons.

"You can sleep dry here, comrades," he said. "I built this place while I was hunting monkey-meat. I do not think the men from the town will come to this river until tomorrow — the darkness is coming. If they should come, they will not find you here."

"Be careful that they do not find you either, friend," Pedro answered.

"They will not find us. If they do they will be sorry,"

He spoke with a calm strength that made me think what a difference a few hours had made in him. That morning he had been a blubbering boy. Now, with the knowledge that Bella was his own and that he could thrash any two of those *caboclos* who had made his life and hers so wretched, he was a man. Rather slow of thought, perhaps, but able to take care of himself from this time on — that was the new Deodoro who now talked so surely and called us "comrades." His eye was steady and his head was up, and he feared no man.

"I am sorry that I had to drive you out in such a way," he went on. "You are the first men who ever did anything for me, and you have done the greatest thing any man could do for me. So I do not like to seem ungrateful, even though you understand and know that I am not. If ever I can do anything for you, Pedro and Lourenço, call on me and I will do it, not matter what it is."

He grinned again.

"That was a very wise plan of yours, Pedro — you know women better than I do. But Bellie nearly spoiled it all when she jumped at Lourenço. I almost forgot everything you had told me to say and do."

"So did I," admitted my partner, "After she did that it was not really necessary to talk about the women I had abandoned — ha ha ha! I nearly laughed in your face. But she is all yours now, friend. Treat her well — but be strong and bold, strong and bold!"

"I will," the Tapir promised earnestly. "*Adeos!*"

He stepped back into his canoe and left us. Pedro took cartridges from a pocket and reloaded his rifle.

THE SILVER AGE OF PULP REPRINTS?

by Mike Chomko

When most people consider the 1960s, they think of Vietnam, student protests, race riots, hippies, drugs, rock 'n roll, and the sexual revolution. But for those of us *Adventure Tales* readers who are pushing fifty and beyond, it was the golden age of the pulp reprint.

I was all of twelve years old in March 1968, when Lyndon Johnson decided not to seek another term as the president of the United States. On the last day of that month, LBJ announced that he would not run again and I could have cared less. What had me worried was how Doc Savage and his men were going to save Prosper City from the Green Bell, better remembered as *The Czar of Fear*

I had discovered Doc and his five fearless friends in the book section at a local department store. The first three titles that I purchased from the series — *Brand of the Werewolf, The Land of Terror,* and *Quest of Qui* — cost me all of 45¢ each. That seems like next to nothing today, but I had to do a lot of arm-twisting to coax a buck-and-a-half out from my father's all-too-slender wallet. Little did he know that those three tales would lead his son to a part-time career as a bookseller, fanzine editor, and occasional writer.

We didn't often get back to that department store, but thankfully, Yeager's Pharmacy stocked the Doc books in one of the wire spinner racks that stood in the store. As the years passed, Doc's price rose until it eventually cracked the dollar mark. Fortunately, my weekly allowance kept pace and I was able to keep lining up one after another of the books in the series.

Whenever I purchased a new "Fantastic Adventure of Doc Savage by Kenneth Robeson," I'd look at the fine print on the contents page. There I would read, "Originally published in *Doc Savage Magazine*" and a date from the 1930s or 40s would be listed. I didn't think at the time that such magazines still existed and that people scattered across the United States, Canada, and other countries collected them, bought them, sold them, and traded them. After all, whenever we had a stack of magazines in the house, my father, a product of the Great Depression and the Second World War, tied them together, hauled them down to Blinderman's, and sold them for a nickel or two. So I was clueless that Doc Savage had once appeared in what was called a pulp magazine.

Richard Nixon was inaugurated as our 37th president in January of 1969, but of far more importance to one bespectacled lad, growing up in a small town in eastern Pennsylvania, was his introduction to "the Shadow" during the summer of that year. After years of success with the Doc Savage franchise, Bantam Books had decided to revive yet another pulp character, one whose original pulp adventures predated those of the good doctor by nearly two years.

Probably due to its unglamorous cover art, the Shadow never took off for Bantam. However, the genie had escaped from its bottle and other pulp heroes began to turn up in the spinner rack at my home town drugstore — R. T. M. Scott's and Norvell Page's Spider, Robert J. Hogan's G-8, Paul Ernst's Avenger, and Robert E. Howard's Conan, immortalized through Frank Frazetta's cover art for the Lancer paperback series. Many other pulp characters never made it to Yeager's bookrack — Dusty Ayres, Secret Agent X, the Phantom Detective, Tarzan of the Apes, John Carter of Mars, Operator #5, Edmond Hamilton's Captain Future, and others. Those grand old serials from *Argosy* and other pulp magazines, fine-tuned by the editorial pen of Donald A. Wollheim, likewise never found their way to my hometown. Nor did the science fiction and fantasy from *Astounding Stories, Startling Stories, Weird Tales,* and other classic pulp magazines, reborn in paperback format, find many spots on that spinner rack. Although Max Brand and his mythical cowboys and Indians were often present, it would be a couple of decades before I came to appreciate the work of Frederick Faust and his supermen of the West. The same can be said about the tough guy dicks created by such *Black Mask* stalwarts as Dashiell Hammett and Raymond Chandler.

Few of the aforementioned series lasted very long. Conan and the tarnished knights of Hammett and Chandler have endured, finding homes not only on library shelves, but also in comic books, movies, and other mediums. Ernst's *Avenger* series that, like *Doc Savage*, was credited to Kenneth Robeson, was reprinted in its entirety by Warner. About half of Hamilton's thrilling adventures of Curt Newton were resurrected as paperbacks by Popular Library while twenty-plus *Phantom Detective* yarns were knocked out by Corinth Books, a pornography publisher with limited distribution channels. And Jim Hatfield of *Texas Rangers* again roamed the West as a paperback hero.

The late sixties and early seventies were a pulp fan's dream. Although series came and went, it seemed almost as if the pulps had been born again in the cheap paperback format that had partially brought about their demise. However, as the seventies wore on, many of those who had once enjoyed the paperback exploits of Doc and the Shadow, Tarzan and Conan, Captain Future and Northwest Smith, moved on, entering college and losing interest in or becoming too busy for the adventures that had once thrilled them. Gradually, the market for such books diminished, and attempts to revive such characters for the mass market fell flat. Eventually, even Doc Savage, after his entire oeuvre had been reprinted, disappeared from the bookshelves and spinner racks of stores across America. For pulp fans, it had been a golden age, but it was over.

Like many others, my interest in pulp fiction waned during the late seventies and early eighties. I was busy with "real life" — college, my first job, marriage, and so on. I did, however, remain a reader, but one with more "refined" tastes. Then, for some reason or other, I again began to dabble in pulp fiction. This time I was hooked.

The late eighties was a time when, although very few of the stories that had once filled the magazines of America's newsstands were being reissued, much was being written about those very same stories. In Tom and Ginger Johnson's *Echoes*, Howard Hopkins' *Golden Perils*, John Gunnison's *The Pulp Collector*, and other publications, the pulps were being seriously explored by writers such as Nick Carr, Shawn Danowski, Don Hutchison, Will Murray, Robert Sampson, and Albert Tonik. The offspring of Lynn Hickman's *The Pulp Era*, Fred Cook's *Bronze Shadows*, and Nils Hardin's *Xenophile*, these amateur magazines were a treasure trove of information about the magazines and the people who had created the world of pulp fiction. They would, in turn, give rise to a new age of the pulp reprint — that in which we are currently living — the reprint's silver age.

It probably began in 1988, when Doug Ellis launched *Pulp Vault*, a magazine of pulp fact and fiction. Ellis blended nonfiction articles about the pulps with reprints of the fiction that his authors were discussing. In his initial issue, Peter the Brazen, the first "man of bronze," battled the Blue Scorpion in "The Sapphire Death." It had originally been serialized in the pages of *Argosy*.

Later that same year, Camille Cazedessus revived *The Fantasy Collector*, an amateur magazine where pulp fans had bought, traded, and sold the magazines they loved. Like Ellis, Cazedessus blended fact with fiction, but his forte was the fantastic. The first issue of *The Fantasy Collector* began a serialization of "A

Son of the Stars," a "long lost fantasy story" written by Frank Aubrey. Eventually, Cazedessus would rename his magazine *Pulpdom*. It is still being published and continues to mix fact and fiction.

For the die-hard pulp fan such as I had become, both *Pulp Vault* and *The Fantasy Collector* were most welcome. However, they had their limitations, primarily their scanty distribution.

It was in December of 1991 that John Gunnison, publisher of *The Pulp Collector*, launched a new magazine. It was called *Pulp Review*. The first issue was sixteen pages long and came in a cardstock cover with a black-and-white illustration. The issue was given away as a free sample and was hoped to be the first of many issues that would reprint the fiction from those grand old pulp magazines. Following a one-page editorial that described the magazine's format, detailed advertising rates, and announced a publication schedule, Gunnison reprinted a Dan Turner story from the pages of *Spicy Detective*. Following this first issue, on a bimonthly basis, Gunnison returned with more pulp fiction.

The next five issues of *Pulp Review* followed the first issue's format — cardstock covers featuring a black-and-white illustration with interiors reproduced directly from the pulps. Beginning with its seventh issue, *Pulp Review* added a glossy cover, but still reproduced a black-and-white illustration. A year later, it added color to its covers. Finally, at the end of 1995, *Pulp Review* became *High Adventure*, the name it continues to use after nearly fifteen years of continuous publication. Gunnison's magazine is now distributed by Diamond Comic Distributors on a nationwide basis.

Although several other small publishers, including Cazedessus and Tom and Ginger Johnson, have reprinted a large amount of pulp fiction, it was John Gunnison's *Pulp Review/High Adventure* that demonstrated that there was a specialized marketplace for such material. His magazine paved the way for the revival of the pulp reprint market.

Today a fairly large number of mostly small publishers are digging through the pulp magazines of the early twentieth century and bringing back a wide variety of fiction for the modern reader. Gunnison's Adventure House continues to publish *High Adventure* on a bimonthly basis. It also reprints *G-8 and His Battle Aces* on a quarterly schedule and will soon begin issuing about six pulp facsimiles every three months. According to Gunnison, the titles will be "spread from the saucy to the fantastic — whatever strikes my fancy and remains in the public domain."

After the success of its three-volume set that reprinted the complete adventures of psychic detective Jules de Grandin from the pages of *Weird Tales*, Battered Silicon Dispatch Box of Ontario began a new series entitled *Lost Treasures from the Pulps*. Although these volumes are fairly expensive, they reprint some very entertaining material including the complete Peter the Brazen, Moon Man, and Don Diablo series from the pulps. Several of Battered Silicon's volumes have delved into the pages of *Dime Detective Magazine*, one of the best of the detective pulps, and brought back some extremely enjoyable tales.

Bold Venture Press, based in New Jersey, is the new home for *The Spider*, regarded as one of the greatest of the pulp heroes. Bold Venture hopes to release at least four Spider adventures this year. Recently, it also issued a collection that reprinted the complete adventures of the Domino Lady, a saucy debutante who dabbles in crime solving.

Girasol Collectables, another Canadian publisher, issues three pulp facsimiles each month. Although they cost $25-35 each, Girasol's "Pulp Replicas" reprint some of the premier pulp magazines of the early twentieth century — *Horror Stories*, *Operator #5*, *Oriental Stories*, *Spicy Detective*, *The Spider*, *Terror Tales*, *Weird Tales*, and others.

Wildside Press, publisher of the magazine you hold in your hands, is also one of the leading publishers of the new pulp revival. In addition to *Adventure Tales*, Wildside has a series of pulp facsimiles of many different pulp magazines including *Black Mask*, *Ghost Stories*, *Sinister Stories*, and *Submarine Stories*. How's that for variety? Their Pulp Classics feature single-author collections drawn from the pulps. For those who enjoy the hero pulps, Wildside has three series — *Operator #5*, *The Phantom Detective*, and *Secret Agent X*. They have also been reprinting the work of Robert E. Howard, including his complete work for *Weird Tales*.

There are many other independent publishers releasing books culled from the pages of those crumbling old magazines that we hold so dear. In future columns, I hope to highlight some of the best of the books being published in this silver age of the pulp reprint. In the meantime, if you're in the market for such books, please look for my advertisement elsewhere in this issue. My bookselling specialty is pulp-related books.

by Our Readers

Recently I received the first issue of *Adventure Tales* from Mike Chomko. I was delighted with the contents especially your trying to put a little history of the authors in it. Your choice of stories was good except for "The Spider Strain." I can't stand the speech of the main character, John Warwick.

A while ago I stumbled on an interesting boxing story. I don't know if you are interested. If you like, I can make a copy and send it to you.

Al Tonik

Thanks for the offer. I'd be happy to take a look at the boxing story (and anything else you'd care to send). Please drop it in the mail!

"The Spider Strain" was a little more dated than most of our contents, I do admit. However, I felt justified in including it because it's part of one of those legendary series people read about all the time, but never actually encounter. I will admit that I much prefer Johnston McCulley's other series, especially Thubway Tham (my current favorite!)

— Editor

CLASSIC PULP FICTION FROM WILDSIDE PRESS!

Satan's Daughter and Other Tales from the Pulps
by E. Hoffman Price. Intro by Darrell Schweitzer

A baker's dozen of classic pulp stories, by a master of the genre! *Satan's Daughter and Other Tales from the Pulps* includes such rare gems as the title story, "Scourge of the Silver Dragon," "Revolt of the Damned," "Pit of Madness," "The Walking Dead," "Drink or Draw," and many more. A delightful selection, ranging from fantasy to horror to action-mystery, all sprinkled with a dash of erotica.

Out of the Wreck and Other Nautical Tales
by Captain A. E. Dingle

Captain A.E. Dingle published sea stories in the pulp magazines for decades, and the volume, quality and variety of his tales is nothing short of astonishing. This collection assembles eight of his finest, from the Sherlock Holmes pastiche "Watson!" to the short novel "The Coolie Ship," from the misadventures of "Skimps, Ship's Boy" to the lives of "Hard-Shell Clammers" -- nautical stories told by a master craftsman!

The Mysterious Wu Fang: Case of the Suicide Tomb
by Robert J. Hogan

The ancient tomb had been sealed for a thousand years; its discovery was an archaeological find. But few guessed its horrible secret, or knew that an Oriental super-villain, the fiendish Wu Fang, wished to enter its portals to capture the death germs buried there -- deadly germs of a rare plague of madness which he meant to use to control the world! From the December, 1935 issue of *The Mysterious Wu Fang* magazine, presented with its original cover and interior art.

Operator #5: Blood Reign of the Dictator
by Curtis Steele

Operator #5 appeared in more than 48 novels in the pulp magazine bearing his name. From April 1934 to November 1939, Jimmy Christopher fought villains from inside the United States and invaders from without. With World War II looming on the horizon, the Operator #5 books became a reflection of the times -- none more so than when a fascist dictator appears to take over the U.S. government! *Blood Reign of the Dictator* is a classic entry in the series.

Secret Agent "X": The Legions of the Living Dead
by Brant House

From the September, 1935 issue of *Secret Agent X* comes this sensational novel: "From nowhere hurtled that black death car. And from nowhere came its grisly occupants. They were not of the earth, for their human flesh was immune to bullets. They were not of the grave, for they manned the wheel and a blasting machine gun- Secret Agent "X" made a desperate maneuver to block their invasion of the land of the living. And in that weird terror trap, he came face to face with a man he knew had died five years ago!"

PURE PULP FICTION!

The Maker of Gargoyles, by Clark Ashton Smith
600-copy hardcover edition, $29.95.

Clark Ashton Smith was a prodigy who wrote Arabian Nights novels in his mid teens and was heralded as a major voice in American poetry by the time he was nineteen. In one frantic burst in the middle 1930s, he wrote nearly a hundred strange, wondrous, and grotesque stories, most of which were published in *Weird Tales*, *Strange Tales*, *Wonder Stories*, and other pulps, but he was by no means a conventional pulp writer. A direct heir to Edgar Allan Poe and to the late Romantics and Decadents, Smith wrote in baroque, jeweled prose of distant times and remote planets, of baleful magics and reanimated corpses, lost lovers, eldritch gods, and inexorable fate.

Think of him as the sorcerer-poet, alone in his eyrie in the dry California hills, dreaming his strange dreams and creating his unique worlds—of Zothique, the Earth's haunted last continent at the end of time; Hyperborea, a prehistoric land; Poseidonis, the last foundering isle of Atlantis; and Averoigne, an unhistoried province of medieval France, thick with vampires. Think of the visions his stories conjure up as sendings, written in strange runes, transported from the sorcerer's lair by indescribable genii or winged spirits.

This fine collection of Clark Ashton Smith's work reprints eight of his classic fantasies, including two set in Hyperborea.

OUT OF THE WRECK	SATAN'S DAUGHTER	FAR BELOW	THE BLACK MASK	STRANGE TALES
by Capt. A.E. Dingle	by E. Hoffmann Price	Ed. by Robert Weinberg	(May 1922 - 2nd issue!)	(Jan. 1933 - 7th issue!)
$14.99 (trade pb)	$15.95 (trade pb)	$15.95 (trade pb)	$19.95 (trade pb)	$19.95 (trade pb)
	$40.00 (hardcover)	$35.00 (hardcover)